Reunion for the First Time

by

K.M. Daughters

Reunion for the First Time

Cover Art by *Kim Mendoza*

The Wild Rose Press, Inc.
PO Box 708
Adams Basin, NY 14410-0708
Visit us at www.thewildrosepress.com

Publishing History
First Champagne Rose Edition, 2016
Print ISBN 978-1-5092-0749-7
Digital ISBN 978-1-5092-0750-3

Published in the United States of America

He shook her hand,

just skimming her knuckles with his fingers, a pleasant connection. *So this is the famous Lizzie.* Now he was sorry for not meshing.

Beguiling smile, tender eyes, legs even better close up. On the skinny side, but appealing curves where it counted. Plus she obviously cared about Charlie, and that meant a great deal.

"Oh. Jack finally." She brushed her bangs out of her eyes. "Mari told me so much about you. Nice to meet you."

She bent her head and surveyed the floor.

"Looking for your dog?" He turned toward the back of the house joining in the search.

"Ah, yes. Marty. Marty!" she blasted.

His ears vibrated. The dog tore from behind him toward Lizzie with jubilant owner worship yips. Lizzie scooped up the little dog and let her lick the side of her cheek unhindered. Made Jack want to be a Boston terrier.

Praise for K.M. Daughters

"What a marvelous story."

> *~Coffee Time Romance and More*
> *Reviewer's award*
> *(5 Cups)*

~*~

"Compelling, page turner. Put your worries aside for a few hours and enjoy what this story has to offer."

> *~RT Book Reviews*

Dedication

For Mom and Daddy,
the K and M in K.M. Daughters

Chapter One

Lizzie Moran approached Charlie's brownstone, unlatched the metal gate, and bounded up the steps that led to mahogany double doors, her Boston terrier trotting beside her. Above her head gleamed a gorgeous stained glass window. Beautiful butterflies—*mariposas* in flight—crowned the doors.

"Oh, Mari, I miss you so. Please help me. Help me help him. He's breaking my heart," she whispered.

Wrestling with her own ever-present grief, she took a deep breath to steel her resolve and make another attempt to help Charlie Clark fashion a life without his beloved Mari.

She repositioned the bakery bag in the crook of the same arm that held a two-cup coffee carrier, hitched up the strap on her right shoulder to swing her art portfolio behind her, used the key Mari had given her, and opened the door.

As she let go of the leash, the dog rushed into the dim foyer and then sat—intent on her mistress' face—at the base of the central staircase. Thin rays of morning sunlight came through the stained glass window and spotted the butter colored walls and scuffed wood floors with rainbows.

Lizzie stooped to undo Marty's leash, setting the coffee cups on the floor. She dipped a hand into the bag, broke off a piece of scone, and offered it to the

1

dog. The bribe of buttery pastry was the only way to get her little pet to walk the distance to Charlie's house in Lincoln Park from Lizzie's condo building in River North.

Picking up the coffee carrier, she stuffed the bag under her arm and grabbed the handle of the portfolio with her free hand. "Hey Charlie!"

No answer. She walked farther down the hall and first entered the living room, then the dining room, flinging open the drapes, leaning the portfolio against the sills temporarily at each of the windows.

"Charlie! Where are you?"

He wouldn't answer her. She dropped in as often as she could since Mari's funeral, sometimes daily if she wasn't out of town on assignment. He never welcomed her, although she couldn't allow that to deter her. He obviously needed the love and caring of good friends, even if he was too dispirited to acknowledge it.

Heading toward the great room at the rear of the house, Lizzie entered the kitchen area. She deposited the coffees and pastries on the counter, her usual treats to try to get a smile out of him, slipped the strap off her shoulder and laid the portfolio flat on the kitchen table. Pulling a large manila envelope out of it, she walked into the adjoining family room where Charlie slumped in a chair.

He was unshaven and unkempt. His greasy black hair needed a comb. Little wisps of gray spiked around his crown and stuck to the sides of his face. Dressed in his habitual dull brown bathrobe over navy blue sweat pants, his face smudgy with whiskers, he presented a heart-sinking challenge.

Lizzie placed the envelope on the coffee table and

sat on the sofa across from him.

"Hi, Charlie."

"Yeah, hi."

She wished he'd at least look at her. "Smells funny in here, Charlie. Want me to freshen the place up while you have a shower?"

"No."

"How about some coffee?"

No answer.

She rose and got him a cup, walked over and handed it to him, refusing to let her hopeful intentions be dashed by the wave of dismay that threatened to overwhelm her.

He took the coffee, sipped, and sat there.

"Well." Lizzie moved back to her seat on the sofa. She touched the envelope and noticed her hand shook.

He's making me a nervous wreck.

"I brought you something special today that I think you'll be really excited about."

The last thing he looked was excited. Dull-eyed, slack-jawed, Charlie looked like he was suffering from some fatal disease.

Like Mari. Oh Charlie, giving up won't bring her back.

Lizzie inhaled deeply and soldiered on. "Over the years, I've taken some just-for-fun shots of the most amazing buildings I've ever seen."

She paused hoping for a response. None came. Frustrated, she tucked a strand of hair behind her ear.

"But they're so much more than just buildings, Charlie. They're like giant sculptures that people live and work in. Beautiful art, really. I think they have coffee table book written all over them. You've always

3

wanted to publish a collection of my work. Well, I realize…"

"No." His tone held no warmth, none of its remembered sweetness.

She leaned forward for emphasis, still hopeful that she could get through his depression. "Charlie, I think this is a viable project. It's a complete departure for me to photograph anything other than people. This is perfect for you, and you can get back to work again."

"I'm not going back to work."

She reached over the coffee table and cupped his knee with her hand. "What do you mean you're not going back to work?"

She squeezed his knee. "Charlie, look at me. Please."

He faced her instead of looking at the floor. "I don't want to go back to work."

His obstinate glare depressed her, made her feel helpless. "But they need you, Charlie, to run the company."

"The company's fine without me."

"But…"

"No."

Beyond frustrated Lizzie declared, "I'm so sick of this, Charlie. Life goes on. You *have* to live. Mari would be railing at you in untranslatable Spanish. You're lucky you don't have to face what she'd have to say about your smelly bathrobe and the mess in her house."

"Don't." The word growled out of him, drawing her dog's attention.

The pup scampered over to Charlie's chair and hoisted up on her hind legs, front paws against his thighs, nub tail shimmying back and forth. He held a flat palm toward the dog's lolling tongue, and she lapped it across his hand. He grimaced.

"Marty, get down," Lizzie commanded. The dog obeyed and trotted over to her. Lizzie rewarded her with a loving stroke from the top of the head to her tail while she stared at Charlie.

He had drawn an imaginary line on the floor between them that he wouldn't permit her to cross. More than anger shimmered in his eyes. She gazed into an impenetrable glaze of pain.

Lizzie couldn't deal with her own emotions facing off with his. Bereft, aching for him and near tears missing her sister-of-the heart, Mari, she had nothing left to dig him out of his wife's grave; the book idea was her last attempt.

This whole thing is a big failure.

"Fine." Her tone sounded more aggravated than she wanted. "Sorry to bother you. Gee, don't get up. I'll let myself out."

Lizzie scooped up Marty and held the dog against her hip. A light snow of pastry crumbs littered a trail behind them as Lizzie strode to the table and snatched up her portfolio, slinging the strap over her shoulder. She wanted him to jump up, stop her and tell her to cool down. Even if he used his anger to yell at her, it would be an improvement.

"Okay. Bye," he mumbled, depriving her of any encouraging reaction.

She rushed through the hallway to the foyer, heaved the door open and then pulled up short, her pup snuggled warm against her, licking the back of her hand.

She set the dog down on the floor. "Go give Uncle Charlie another kiss. You can play with him for a while." She petted the dog's back, smiling into those crazy "Marty Feldman" eyes.

"Go ahead, Marty. Go see Charlie. Maybe he has more scone for you."

The dog trotted away. Lizzie left Charlie's house jumping down the steps in twos, still upset about him but optimistic that Marty's hero worship would soothe him.

Dashing through the gate, she veered right toward Lincoln Park. She'd let Marty try to pry a smile out of the man while she walked off her frustration near the lake.

****

Jack Clark walked into the Starbucks. The blast of air conditioning was a welcome relief from the humid heat. With his damp T-shirt sticking to his chest and back, it was great to be super-cooled for a while.

Even though he considered it mild insanity on such a day, he bought two coffees because Charlie loved the stuff hot and frothy. Pushing the shop door open with his back, he ventured out into the ninety-degree steam bath. Armed with the drinks as a social excuse to get in the door, he went to do battle.

Determination pushed him the few blocks to Charlie's house to bring his beloved, albeit hardheaded, older brother back to the land of the living. Six months was long enough to allow his only sibling to remain inert in grief. He'd be damned if he'd sit by and watch Charlie take after their old man.

The brisk, early morning traffic slowed Jack down at intersections. Nearing the outskirts of Lincoln Park, he waited for the line of cars to clear on the corner before Charlie's block. A movement ahead caught his eye.

A woman tore down Charlie's front steps, rounded the gate and headed away from Jack. Snug shorts exposed a nice set of shapely tanned legs. A long brunette ponytail bobbed behind her. If the face matched the rear view, he would have liked the time to catch up with her.

Jack paused in front of the brownstone. For the past few years, it seemed more like home than his condo. Mari had filled it with her special touch and unbridled love. The sister-in-law, and in many ways the mother he'd never had, Mari had welcomed Jack here and melded him into her wide circle of loved ones.

Always a good sport, Mari laughed when he made fun of her accent—you can take the girl out of Guatemala, but you can't take Guatemala out of the girl. She wanted the best for him, which had him evading her incessant matchmaking attempts like a diplomat. He missed her every day.

The glittering collage of butterflies in stained glass over the door drew his attention and he sent a silent prayer to Mariposa to help him snap Charlie back.

Pushing the buzzer with his elbow, he tapped an impatient rhythm with his foot, a coffee cup in each hand.

"Who is it?" came his brother's muffled voice from inside.

Eager to hand over the coffee and have a serious talk with Charlie, Jack boomed, "Hey, Chuck. Open up."

"What are you doing here?"

Talking through a door, feeling stupid standing in the hot sun and praying this isn't a waste of time. "Nice welcome. Open up. I have coffee."

"More coffee, just what I need. This place is turning into a revolving door at Starbucks."

More muffled grumbling could be heard as the door swung open. Jack passed by his brother and into the hermit's lair, just like Dad's place. He shivered at the memory.

As boys, they had watched the life seep out of their father after their mother took off for another man's greener pasture. Still a cheerless, passionless man, Dad had raised them well enough with a lot of help from their maternal grandfather. When Jack thought of the father-son events of his life, he always thought of his grandfather, not his Dad. He'd chip away at Charlie forever before he let him turn into their father.

"Did a woman just leave here?" Jack continued to walk through the house to the living room looking over his shoulder to see if his brother was following.

"What woman?" Charlie stood by the open door and looked at him dull-eyed.

"Slim brunette? Nice legs?"

"None of your business." Charlie shuffled toward the back of the house. He still wore his pajamas, and his hair was filthy.

Jack hardly recognized his brother who used to dress like a GQ model.

"What the hell are you doing hibernating in your bathrobe all day?" Jack put the coffee cups down on the hall table and reversed direction to close the door.

"Geez, let some light in." He went from window to window in the front of the house and tugged open the drapes suspecting the curtains wouldn't stay open long. Maybe two minutes after he left Charlie alone.

Catching up with his brother at the entrance to the great room, Jack walked, more like shuffled at his brother's pace, at Charlie's elbow. "Time to get moving. Today is the start of the rest of your life."

"Yeah, Tony Robbins." Charlie turned away from him and moved toward the family room. "I'm not interested. Thanks for the coffee. Feel free to leave any time."

"Not until you hear me out." Jack paced inches away from his heels. "I have a proposition for you."

A brown and white dog trotted toward Jack with a flurry of nail clicks on the hardwood floor. He stooped down and petted it. "Whoa, what's this?"

The small terrier wagged its nub tail and rolled over in belly-offering submission.

Charlie plopped down in the nearest chair. "A dog."

"Got that part, wise guy." Jack took a seat facing him. "You get a dog? Good idea if you ask me."

"Lizzie brought it here. I'm everybody's project today."

The dog jumped straight into Charlie's lap, turned a half circle and curled up in a ball.

"Is that who I saw racing down your steps? Mari's friend Lizzie?"

"Yeah." Charlie didn't bend his head or acknowledge the animal despite the racket from the dog's buzz saw snores. But his face softened—a small scrap of amusement in his brother's mournful world.

"You know the ball my company sponsors every year for charity?" Jack knew this was going to be hard, but man, Charlie didn't budge an inch.

"I called my lawyer yesterday and put her to work to establish us as Co-Chairs of The Mariposa Leukemia Foundation. The ball will be held in memory of our Mari this year and every year from now on. I need your help with this. I can't do it alone." Jack cringed at what the mere mention of Mari's name did to his brother. It was hard on him, too. He loved her like a sister.

Charlie folded over with the onslaught of grief. The dog wiggled and contorted from under the canopy of Charlie's body, planted its hind legs on the chair cushion and laved its tongue over the side of Charlie's grief-contorted face.

Sobs rasped out of him, and his torso quaked as he pushed the dog down into his lap. "I can't." Charlie's voice sounded wet and guttural as if his lips were submerged in water.

Choked gasps echoed through the house.

Jack knelt in front of Charlie's chair and wrapped his arms around him and the dog. "Charlie, you can. You know you can. Think. What would Mari want you to do?"

How had he shrunk so much? Charlie's ribs protruded beneath Jack's hands, and his own arms looked huge compared to his brother's. It killed him that his brother was wasting away. He had to save him.

After a few minutes, Charlie relaxed, and the spasms came farther apart, encouraging Jack. The dog slid out from under Jack's arms, jumped down and skittered away.

Jack hugged Charlie tighter. "Do you think Mari would be happy to see you make a cave out of her home and defile the life you made together? What about

Butterfly Books? Do you think it will run itself forever? Are you just going to let it fold?"

Releasing the embrace, Jack eased back on his heels. He gazed directly into Charlie's bloodshot eyes, hoping he could capitalize on the fact that Charlie didn't have enough energy to break the force field of his gaze.

"I've tried to be patient, Charlie, tried to respect your enormous loss. But I lost my sister. I lost our parents when Mom took off and Dad became the way he is. I can't lose my brother, too. I won't lose my brother. Butterfly Books needs you. I need you. What will it take to bring you back? What can I do to help you?"

Charlie stared at Jack with glazed blue eyes, shrugged and said nothing.

Jack straightened. He had to move otherwise he would break something, like Charlie's bones. Pacing back and forth, he kept his distance. Picking up an envelope on the coffee table, he debated his next maneuver.

"What's this?" Jack held it in under Charlie's down-turned eyes.

"I don't know. Lizzie was all fired up about it. I didn't pay attention."

"Pissing off everybody, aren't you, Charlie?"

Jack opened the manila envelope's flap and spilled its contents onto the marble tabletop. "What the hell? I didn't know you had Lizzie Moran taking pictures of my buildings."

Jack had heard about Elizabeth Moran, the celebrated photojournalist and former member of the Peace Corps. She had met Mari in Guatemala working on some engineering project. Charlie did a stint in the Peace Corps, too, and the three of them linked up there. Jack had never met Mari's friend. Their schedules never meshed. Not meshing their schedules was on purpose. Mari, never subtle, wanted to play Cupid and he had no idea if Lizzie went along with it or even knew. Either way, Jack avoided anyone's meddling in his social life, even his beloved Mari's.

"Lizzie never took any pictures for me. Are you ready to leave now? I'm really tired." Charlie yawned widely.

"Tired from what? All that effort from ignoring me?"

Jack stalked toward Charlie and thrust a fistful of photos under his nose. "These are mine. My designs. What are you and Elizabeth Moran doing with them? Take a look."

"For God's sake. If I look at them, will you leave?"

"If you look at them, I won't kill you."

Charlie stood and grabbed the prints out of Jack's hand. He shuffled through them once and then again slower.

Jack watched his brother's subtle change, the dawn of professional interest, a glimmer of blessed animation in Charlie's face.

Thank you, God and Elizabeth.

"These are very good." Charlie handed the photos back to Jack with a jerk of his arm. "There, I looked at them."

Jack ignored the dismissal. He had Charlie talking and moving around. Excitement made his heart beat faster. "Good? They're spectacular, the composition, the light, and night shots. She's honored each design.

Why did she bring them here?"

"I guess she wanted me to do a coffee table book of these prints. Something about how she took these shots in her travels." Charlie rocked from foot to foot in the sheepish, guilty dance Jack remembered from when they were caught mischief-making as kids.

"I was pretty awful to her. She left in a huff."

"Gee, and I think you're so darned charming."

"Yeah, well." Charlie pulled on his hair and grimaced at the greasy smear on his fingers. "I think I could use a shower."

Afraid to say anything that might deflate the fragile balloon of hope that filled Jack, he nodded. He stood and watched his brother walk away.

Charlie's footsteps thudded up the stairs, and Jack's eyes brimmed with tears. He walked down the hall, stopped at the foot of the stairs and drummed his fingers on the smooth grooves of the carved mahogany banister.

"Hey, Chuck!" he hollered.

"Yeah," Chuck's voice resonated with life—a voice that Jack hadn't heard in a long time. He laid his head on the banister with relief.

"I'm hungry. Are you up for Lou Malnati's on Wells? I could eat a large deep-dish all by myself." Jack held his breath.

"I'm hungry, too…"

Great. That's a good sign.

"Maybe order delivery. Give me ten minutes."

A flow of water echoed hollow through the pipes and Jack let out his breath with a *whoosh*.

It was a start.

As he turned away to go take another look at those

pictures, the front door burst inward toward Jack. Jumping back before it clocked him, he lost his balance as the female that followed quickly through the door did clock him in a soft collision of breasts against his chest.

"Ohmygosh, I'm so sorry." Standing in front of him, a pretty blush spread on her lightly tanned cheeks.

"No problem…miss?" He backed up to give her space, shoving the front door closed.

"Lizzie Moran." She held out a hand. "And you are?"

"Jack Clark." He shook her hand, just skimming her knuckles with his fingers, a pleasant connection. *So this is the famous Lizzie.* Now he was sorry for not meshing.

Beguiling smile, tender eyes, legs even better close up. On the skinny side, but appealing curves where it counted. Plus she obviously cared about Charlie, and that meant a great deal.

"Oh. Jack finally." She brushed her bangs out of her eyes. "Mari told me so much about you. Nice to meet you."

She bent her head and surveyed the floor.

"Looking for your dog?" He turned toward the back of the house joining in the search.

"Ah, yes. Marty. Marty!" she blasted.

His ears vibrated. The dog tore from behind him toward Lizzie with jubilant owner worship yips. Lizzie scooped up the little dog and let her lick the side of her cheek unhindered. Made Jack want to be a Boston terrier.

"Cute dog." He couldn't help but look at those legs.

"Thanks. Where's Charlie?" She nudged the dog away from her face.

"Taking a shower." Finally getting Charlie up and about brought a smile to his face.

"No kidding?" Her deep green eyes widened to twice their size. "What did you do, club him and prop him up under the water?"

Jack laughed. "No. But it crossed my mind."

She turned toward the open door. "I have to run. Tell Charlie I came back for Marty?"

"Sure," he agreed following her toward the door.

"Nice to finally meet you, Jack. And, thank you for whatever you did to make the difference with Charlie. I've been knocking my head against the wall trying to get through to him." She smiled and turned slowly toward the street.

"Same here." He stood and watched her walk the dog down the block. Mari, bless her heart, might have been on to something.

Jack closed the door and headed to the den, Mari on his mind. She had hounded him to meet Elizabeth Moran because they had so much in common.

He picked up the photos Lizzie had left behind. Color, black and white, even night shots from unique perspectives—her sheer artistry impressed Jack. Her looks impressed him, too, enough to arouse his curiosity about the woman Mari had so loved.

But Mari wanted everyone to have true love, the kind that came with marriage licenses and browsing furniture showrooms. She had wanted that for him. Scared him senseless.

Creaks and footfalls overhead, "Hey Jack!"

Jack hurried back to the stairs and saw Charlie on

the upper landing, a towel wrapped around his waist.

God, he's thin.

"I've been meaning to ask you, how did you do on that bid you were telling me about a while ago?" Charlie rubbed a towel over his wet hair.

Stunned, that in his catatonic state, Charlie had apparently listened to him, Jack worked to keep the tone of his voice even, "Great. I got the contract to design the Freedom Center in Boston. Beat out the Prescott Group in its own backyard. It's about time, too. That Prescott is an embarrassment to the industry. Are you going to publish the coffee table book, Charlie?" Jack prayed Lizzie's photos had hooked Charlie, too.

"The works of the illustrious architect JP Hamilton? I don't know. I might."

Chapter Two

The phone rang inside her condo, and Lizzie fumbled with her keys. She juggled the cumbersome portfolio on her shoulder and tried to maintain balance while Marty tugged on the leash.

Lizzie had muttered disgruntled epithets about Charlie the whole way home. The dog could always pick up on her moods. As soon as Lizzie shoved the front door open, Marty yanked away and ran under the bed where she kept a stash of toys.

Lizzie dropped everything on the carpet to the right of the door and nudged it shut with an elbow jab while she slid across the kitchen tile to nab the phone before it stopped ringing.

"Hello?" She leaned against the kitchen counter breathing hard.

"Hi, Lizzie. I thought I was on my way to your voicemail." The familiar Boston accent, the sound of loving friendship.

"Kay, hi. It's so good to hear your voice. How are you feeling?"

"I imagine the same way a beached whale must feel in ninety degree sand."

"Oh, you poor thing. Why doesn't Mick just get someone to install central air in that old barn to make your pregnancy easier on you?"

"Don't get me started. Mick wants to do the

renovations himself. He's doing a beautiful job…wait 'til you see. But he's gotten busy at work and hasn't had the time to finish the house. I'm sitting here feeling sorry for myself." She huffed out a sigh. "I wanted to talk to my best friend and invite you to my pity party."

"Perfect. I'll win hands down." Lizzie cradled the phone between her ear and shoulder, slid a Diet Coke out of the refrigerator, popped it open and took a long grateful swig.

"Don't be so sure," challenged Kay. "I'll win the pity prize today."

Ready to engage in the tradition that had started their freshman year as college roommates, Lizzie took first stab at the prize. "I'm so frustrated. I'm afraid I wasted an entire morning with Charlie. I was so sure he'd like my idea." She gulped her drink.

"What idea? How's he doing? I think about him all the time. He's got to be miserable."

"Yeah, he's miserable all right. That's why I was there this morning. I must be naïve, but I thought if I could get him excited about doing a book with me, he'd go back to work and stop being a hermit."

"Are you writing a book?"

"No, no, nothing like that. I have some photos that I took for fun, enough to fill up a coffee table book. You know Charlie's been hounding me to work together with him on a project for years." Lizzie drained the soda can and paced between her kitchen and living room. "He was so passive aggressive. Wouldn't even look at the photos. He virtually kicked me out of the house."

"What did he say?" Kay asked in a soft voice.

"Almost nothing." Lizzie sighed. "That's the point.

18

He's such a thick Irishman. All he did was grunt no. I'm not proud of myself, but I lost my patience and left."

"Don't worry, sweetie. He'll come around."

"There *are* some encouraging signs that he might. I left Marty behind for a half hour or so while I walked off some of my frustration. When I went back to get her, his brother told me he was taking a shower. I'm afraid to get too hopeful but…"

"You see?" Kay's voice was hearty with optimism. "It's a really good sign."

A comfortable silence between them, Lizzie let Kay's assurances sink in and take hold. With the sun-shimmered Chicago River forty floors below, she stared out the windows only half-seeing the city in which her condo was suspended. Her disposition had improved, but helping Charlie was a bust. At least her earlier anger had faded.

She smiled as if she could see the patient, sweet expression on Kay's face that had always been there for her when she needed it. "I'm hogging all the pity. Your turn in the contest, Kay."

"Ooh, I can take my turn now? You're going to owe me big time because I am one, pitiful person."

Lizzie laughed. "Go ahead. I'm sorry. You started this party. It should have been your turn first."

"Well. I've gained forty pounds and I'm only in my second trimester. My ankles are swollen. I look like Miss Piggy in high heels. What am I saying? The only shoes I can get on are Scholl's exercise sandals. My picture alone defines the word cranky. No. Change that. The word's crankiest. *And*. The doctor told me this morning that I'm carrying twins. Good Lord in heaven.

19

I don't know whether to laugh or cry."

"Twins? Oh my God. Kay, that's amazing. This is wonderful. What did the doctor say?"

"He hovered a bit and didn't like my blood pressure readings. I've got some instructions to follow. And for sure he wants to do a C-section when they're big enough. No big deal. My doctor's very good. I trust him."

"Promise you'll follow those orders, okay? I can't wait to hold them."

"I'll be good. And I can't wait to hold them, either. Because then they'll be out of me."

Kay's infectious, healthy laugh reassured her. If anyone could handle what might be a difficult pregnancy, Kay could.

"I'm still in shock, I think…I haven't even told Mick yet. I figured I'd plop some candles on the table and tell him over dinner."

"I know Mick. He'll be over the moon."

"Do you think? Yeah, I think you're right. It is amazing. But I still win."

"Okay. You win. What do you want for a treat?"

"Fannie May chocolates. Any kind. Minimum, two pounds. You can bring them to Boston when you come to the reunion in a few weeks."

"Sneaky. You know you can't drag me to that reunion. The only classmate I care to see from college is you. And thank God we don't need reunions to do that. But I'll gladly Fed Ex the chocolates now that you're eating for three."

"Lizzie, please come. I didn't know I'd be pregnant when I volunteered to run this thing. I'm always so tired, I'm afraid I won't even be able to stay awake for the whole gala. I'll probably keel over snoring into my potatoes duchesse. You've got to come. I need you, Liz."

"Are you going for two boxes of Fannie May? You already won the pity party. I can't take the guilt trip."

"Lizzie, Wallace will be there."

Well, hell.

Lizzie's heart raced and her palms dampened at the prospect of seeing him. "Mother of God, Kay. There's no way I'm going to this thing."

"He's divorced again, honey. Maybe the reunion is a good opportunity for you to put this behind you. Don't you want to know for sure?"

Divorced again. A crazy hope flitted through Lizzie.

Maybe he still loves me. Maybe his marriages have failed because of me.

I can't go there. "I don't think it's a good idea for me to see him again, Kay. Especially alone, and you know I'm not dating anyone. Pathetic, isn't it?"

"Well, how about I fix you up for that weekend? I can think of at least three of Mick's friends who would make good prospects."

Lizzie snorted a laugh. "Now that's appealing. The last time you fixed me up was such fun."

"Ouch. I guess I deserve that. *But* I have apologized many, many times and eaten every kind of crow imaginable, for fixing you up with Wallace in the first place. Look, Lizzie, I think you should face this thing. Either the two of you are meant to be together or you're not. I hope not, because I haven't forgiven him for leaving you without a word on graduation day, even if you have. You'll never move on if you don't resolve this thing with him. Besides, I need your help. Please just come."

How could she deny Kay help? "I promise if I can find a date, I'll come. And I'll ship the Fannie May tomorrow anyway."

The call waiting tone sounded. "Oops, another call. I'll talk to you soon. Love you, Kay."

"Love you, too. *Ciao, Bella.*"

Lizzie fumbled with the buttons on the cell phone. *Stupid thing.* "Hello? Hello?"

"Lizzie?"

The raspy voice on the other end registered. "Charlie?"

It can't be. He hadn't called her in six months. All communication with him had been one-way.

"Yeah, it's Charlie. Listen, Liz. I'm a real jerk. I'm sorry for the way I acted this morning and the past couple of months. You don't deserve it. I know you're trying to help me. I think your photos are great. Maybe we *can* work on a book together sometime soon."

"Wait a minute. Who are you and what have you done with Charlie Clark?"

He chuckled. "Funny girl. I am sorry. For everything. I owe you, Liz. Forgive me?"

"Forgiven. And I think there's a way you can repay me for all the abuse you've shoveled out."

"Name it. Flowers every day, an endless supply of Starbucks. Nothing is too good for you."

"I just might take you up on all that." She laughed, giddy that he had taken the initiative to dial the phone. "But if you're feeling generous, how about coming to Boston with me to my ten-year college reunion?"

"I've never gone to my own reunion. Have I been

that big a problem that this is the only way to make it up to you?"

She was tempted to tell him that he had scared her so much she had considered arranging an intervention with a mental health professional. Lizzie didn't blame him for his recent behavior, but she didn't feel guilty asking him to go to the reunion to "make it up to her", either.

"Kay needs me to go to this thing. And I need a date. Wallace will be there and you know enough of that sad story to understand why I can't face him alone. Please, Charlie. I wouldn't ask if I weren't desperate." Plus, this would get him out, and she could keep an eye on him. He needed to be in social situations. Her poor Charlie.

Dead silence, then, "OK..." He sounded like she had asked him to face a firing squad. "When is it?"

Lizzie couldn't believe her luck. "Wow, thanks, Charlie. It's the first weekend in October."

"That's over a month away." He sounded optimistic. "You'll have time to find someone else to go with you instead."

"Doubt it. I'll be on assignment in Africa and then to Central America. I'll pay for everything, Charlie. I promise we'll have a good time. Kay and Mick are a lot of fun."

"I'm not sure you can count on me. But I'll do it for you. And I wouldn't think of letting you pay. As I said I owe you." Charlie's voice cracked with emotion. "Thanks again for the idea for the book. I'm very grateful. I love you, Elizabeth Moran."

His affectionate tone brought tears to her eyes. "I love you, too, Charles Clark. I'll call you when I get back."

"Be careful wherever you go, okay? Maybe pack a weapon."

"Ha! My press pass is my shield. That, and the military guards I always obey to the letter. I'll keep my eyes open. I always do."

Possibly opening up a wound again, she continued, "I'm going to visit the orphanage after I'm through with this assignment. I want to keep the annual tradition going."

Inhaling deeply she held her breath waiting for his reaction. Her shoulders tightened.

"Right…" His voice barely above a whisper. "Should be plenty hot there this time of year. Travel safe. Tell Becca I said hello."

"Sure. I'll talk to you when I get home." Hanging up the phone, Lizzie exhaled, relieved.

God, it's good to have a normal conversation with him.

Lizzie stepped toward the bank of windows in her living room. She stared at the patch of Lake Michigan visible between the steel and concrete forest of buildings. A single, tiny white sail full of wind moved on the blue waters in front of the Gary, Indiana smoke stacks, which smeared the sky on the far shore ash gray.

Metal screeched as the el train's brakes clenched and held below her. A parade of boats glided on the river, and a serenade of warning bells clanged as metal bridges opened and closed to let taller vessels through.

Despite the constant noise of the city, living in her condo in the clouds always calmed her.

With Charlie's help, maybe seeing Wallace was a good thing.

Chapter Three

Jack checked the time and drummed his fingers on the edge of Charlie's desk. Never able to sit still for long, he stood and paced in front of the window while Charlie made a phone call. Tapping his wristwatch a few times, he widened his eyes and fixed a pointed stare at Charlie just in case his brother hadn't figured out by now how impatient he was to get going.

"Sorry Jack. No answer on her cell phone. It's not like Lizzie to be late." Charlie held the phone toward Jack.

"Well, bro, the lady has fifteen more minutes to show before I'm out of here. I have to go over the plans for the Global Commerce Building." Jack continued to pace around the room.

"I'm so proud of you. The drawings you showed me are awesome. I knew you would be awarded the bid." His brother hung up the phone and leaned back in his large leather chair.

"Haven't gotten it yet. You're thinking of the Freedom Center in Boston. The stakes for the GC Building are the same. We're up against the same firm. I can't tell you how much I want this one, too. It would be very satisfying to beat them out again. The head guy is a real jerk and does shoddy work." Jack's stomach twisted at the thought that his unscrupulous competitor could win this bid.

"I guess you'll be spending a lot of time in Boston."

"Guess so. I'll be back and forth for the next two years, but I'll still be here the majority of the time."

"Are you going back again soon?"

"Why the sudden interest in my travel plans?"

"I want to ask you a favor."

"Sure. Go ahead and ask."

Charlie hesitated. He still had a pleasant smile on his face that had Jack smiling back at him in encouragement. *Oh Charlie, you're not fooling me.* He was too thin, almost frail, and the dark circles under Charlie's eyes made him look worn out despite his clean-shaven face and crisp pale blue shirt.

Look what happens when you give your heart to a woman, Charlie.

Jack banished the mental picture of their father's grim face. At least Charlie was capable of masking his pain with a smile. Dad had never thought his sons deserved the effort.

Determined to do whatever necessary to keep Charlie from falling into the same gray existence, Jack spurred Charlie on, "Anything for you. What do you need?"

Charlie gave him a shaky grin. "I think you better hear the favor before you agree."

"How bad it could it be?" Jack furrowed his brow and chuckled. "It's legal isn't it?"

"In a moment of gratitude I made a promise to Lizzie, and there's no way I can keep it."

"OK. Why not?"

"Because it's next weekend, and it's too soon. But I can't break the promise. I told her I'd do anything to make up for the way I treated her, and she isn't asking anything unreasonable. It's just that I can't do it, that's all."

"I'm still lost here. What's happening next weekend?"

"I agreed to take her to her college reunion in Boston. I'm not ready to be in a social situation without Mari. I still have to push myself to get dressed each day."

"No big deal. Just tell her you can't make it. She knows what a difficult time you're having. Let her find someone else to take her. Or she could go alone, right?"

"You don't understand. Some guy hurt her back in college and he'll be at the reunion. She doesn't want to go alone."

"What's wrong with her? Why can't she get a date?"

"Don't be stupid!" Charlie pointed to the picture on the credenza behind him. "Look at her. She's beautiful. Any man would jump at the chance to go out with her. She needs someone she can count on for this. Someone she trusts."

"I must be dense. What does this have to do with me?"

"Would you take my place and go with her?"

"Oh come on. You're kidding right? I don't even know her." He eyed Charlie's photo of her, long brown hair, a sprinkling of freckles on pale Irish milky skin, and vivid green eyes. He remembered her long legs in shorts and the soft collision with her at Charlie's.

Anyway. "She's not my type."

"Your type. For gods' sake Jack, I'm not asking you to get involved with her. I'm just asking you to help out someone I care about. Just what exactly is your type of woman?"

"Someone who doesn't need her hand held for starters." Nothing worse than an overly dependent female.

Jack stalked behind Charlie's chair and picked up the framed photo he had pointed out. Lizzie with Mari, Charlie and that must be Becca—the Peace Corps Four as Charlie used to refer to them. He hadn't seen any pictures in Charlie's office when he had stopped by during Charlie's bereavement absence to keep a handle on things. His photos were back. A good sign.

"I like women with more curves." Jack returned the picture to its place and resumed pacing. "You know— like Gina. You met her. She is definitely my type."

"I think Mari gave you her opinion of Gina." A smile lit Charlie's face.

Jack snorted a laugh. "Yeah, no question about that."

He turned away from Charlie's desk and stared out the floor to ceiling windows remembering Mari's vehement assertion that he needed to stop wasting time and find the right woman and settle down. Jack turned back to face Charlie. "Scathing. But like I told Mari, I'm not going to marry Gina. Hell, I'm not going to marry anyone."

Jack knew deep inside his heart that he had never met anyone who made him think in that direction at all. He would gladly endure some loneliness to avoid the far worse pitfalls sadly demonstrated by Dad, and now Charlie. Whether the woman leaves on her own or by fate, marriages don't last.

"Yeah, well, I'm not asking you to marry Lizzie.

She's too good for you anyway."

Jack resisted the bait even though he enjoyed sparring with his brother. "You're probably right. So the lady's on her own for her trip back to the glory days of college."

Charlie raked his hand through his hair. "Hear me out, OK, Jack? Lizzie's parents were killed in a car accident on the way to her graduation. I don't know the whole story, but this guy Prescott dumped her around the same time. Her life fell apart. That's why she joined the Peace Corps according to Mari."

"Prescott? What's his first name?" Jack straightened and edged closer to the desk.

"I've only heard him referred to as Wallace Prescott the Third. Always with the Roman numerals. Sounds like a pompous ass to me. Why?"

Jack's spine stiffened. "You've got me interested now. Small world. How did she ever get mixed up with him?"

"They were both students. As far as I know Lizzie's never been serious about anyone else."

Can't imagine her with a conniver like Prescott.

"I'll do it," Jack blurted out impulsively. "Prescott's the jerk I'm competing against on the GC Building. I've beaten him on the last two bids. I know he thought he had the last project wrapped up, especially in his hometown. Let's just say we're unfriendly competitors. Maybe I understand why she's asking you to hold her hand."

Charlie looked dumbstruck. "Thanks Jack. Really."

"Mari will send lightning bolts down from the heavens if I don't help her "sister". I might enjoy playing the white knight to keep that bastard from hurting her again. Does she mind me filling in for you?"

"I didn't ask her yet. I wanted to talk to you first. I wasn't sure I could convince you to help."

"I'm convinced. Sorry I gave you a hard time. I'll build a business trip around it."

"Sure, but the weekend's on me. It's the least I can do."

"You asked for it. First Class air and a suite at The Charles."

"Already done." Charlie pulled a letter-size paper folded in the middle out of his desk drawer and held it out toward Jack. "Your e-ticket."

Jack moved in, took the paper out of Charlie's hand and unfolded it. The airline itinerary—in his name. Hanging over Charlie's desk, he brushed his fist against Charlie's shoulder in a mock punch. "A little sure of yourself, aren't you, bro?"

Jack tucked the ticket in his briefcase. "Sorry. The lady is out of time for this meeting. I have to run. Call me tonight after you talk to her and let me know the plans for the weekend."

Charlie stood and extended his hand. "Thanks Jack, I really appreciate this."

Jack hugged him over the cluttered desk.

"No problem. You can count on me."

Jack grinned in parting and left Charlie's office. *Wally Prescott—Roman numeral three.*

Chapter Four

In his office Friday morning, instead of on his way to O'Hare to meet Lizzie, Charlie looked out the row of tall windows across from his desk. He prized the company's location on Printers Row with its old-time Chicago neighborhood feel and its brick, turn of the century lo-rises—the perfect place for his boutique, publishing firm. No other way to make a living for him. Proud to be responsible for creating books, he appreciated their permanence, their legacy for the generations.

His staff was handpicked, and he valued each employee as his second family. Slowly they had stopped their sugary, stilted behavior toward him since his comeback to work, and a comfortable camaraderie returned.

The easy relationship he enjoyed with Lizzie had returned lately, too. Maybe he was risking that today, certain she would be furious with him as his plan for this weekend unfolded. If she knew that Jack would be on the flight with her ahead of time, she would have cancelled the trip.

It would have been better to get them together earlier as planned. Had she made the meeting last week, he would have pulled that off.

Charlie had no clue what to expect as a result of his manipulations. Thrown together, would they see stars, hear choirs? He half believed they would after reading Mari's journal entry:

I am making no progress with Jack that's for sure. He is more stubborn than me. Doesn't he know that I'm right about such things? He will not agree to meet my sister no matter what I try. And she's no better. No time, no time, she tells me. Then she gets on a plane and disappears again. Well, my Goodness there's always time for love.

Glad he'd acted on Mari's wishes, he now had a purpose despite his sneaky methods. Jack would probably be pissed at him, too, for throwing him unaware into the path of Lizzie's anger. Although devious, the means to their match-up was righteous and even fateful.

After reading his emails, he brought up his calendar. The day would be full. His assistant brought him a mug of coffee, black and almost bitter, the way he liked it.

"Thanks, Allie. You didn't have to bother."

"No bother. Justin wants to know if you're ready to go over some lay-outs."

"Sure. Tell him I'll be there in a few minutes."

A quick glance at his watch. She should be on her way to the airport right now, the deed done.

Lifting a small, framed photo from his desktop, he peered at it. Mari and Lizzie smiled together in the sunshine. He shifted to look at the only other photograph on his desk and picked it up with his other hand. Jack and he smiled back at him in a similar pose. He brought the two pictures together, frames touching and looked closely at the people who meant the most to him. They belonged with each other.

He recalled the rest of her journal entry as if hearing Mari's voice. *I know they were meant to love each other. And I will not stop pushing until they know it, too.*

Charlie smiled in agreement and looked upward where heaven just might be. "She'll be pissed, Mari. But we finally got the two of them together."

****

Lizzie stood in her closet and took stock of her wardrobe. She couldn't decide between the cool, elegant Vera Wang gown with the matching jacket or the short, skimpy cocktail dress. Designer clothing wasn't normally in her budget, but the gown was a splurge. Beige designer silk or red glitter? Both. Better to over-pack.

Pulling the dresses off the rod, she hung them in the suit bag spread open on her bed. Although a veteran traveler, this weekend posed plenty of packing challenges.

Planned events included a welcome reception at the Varsity Club, a tailgate and football game, a boat ride on the Charles River, and a gala at the Boston Harbor Hotel. No matter how nerve wracking, she had to look sensational for all of them. Damn if Wallace wouldn't look at her twice.

Thankfully, the bag zipped closed. She took a minute to run through her mental checklist again. Done.

According to the kitchen clock, she had less than two hours before flight time to get to O'Hare and meet Charlie.

Please, God, let the Kennedy Expressway be open all the way.

Once parked at the airport and grabbing her stuff

out of the trunk, she power walked through the lot and over the bridge that connected the garage to the terminal building.

Unsure if Charlie would wait for her at the First Class check-in counter or if he decided to meet her at the gate, she itched to get off the slow moving escalator.

No Charlie at the counter. Lizzie sped through the check-in process and headed toward the security area, boarding pass and driver's license in hand. Ten minutes later, she darted down the wide corridor toward the two main concourses for the airline. A fat world globe and a parade of national flags overhead, Lizzie hurried toward the gate farthest out.

Boarding was in progress, so Lizzie stepped in line and boarded the plane. She found her row, surprised at the empty seat next to hers.

Stuffing the thin, red blanket on her seat into the stretchy pouch in front of her, she took a paperback out of her purse and tried to relax. A pleasant flight attendant hovered and passengers bumped along past her. She couldn't concentrate on reading.

Where the heck is Charlie?

She opened her purse and searched for her cell phone, then realized she had forgotten it.

****

Jack preferred to board the plane last; legroom was in short supply for six foot five men like him.

Lizzie blew past him so fast he had lost her in the crowd. He didn't expect his surge of pleasure when he had caught sight of her outside the security area. He would have helped with her bags if she hadn't raced ahead.

Stretching his long legs one last time, he pulled himself out of the plastic chair and walked to the end of the line.

Passing passengers' elbows and legs in the narrow aisle of the airplane, Jack stopped next to Lizzie, already belted in the oversized leather seat in the last row of the First Class cabin.

He stowed his duffle bag in the bin over her head. "Hi. Want me next to the window?" He hoped she'd say no.

"Um? Yes." She didn't look up, but tucked her legs to the side to let him cross in front of her. Lizzie kept glancing sideways at the vacant seat across the aisle to her left.

Angling one leg in front of her to straddle her seat, he bent close out of necessity. Her fresh floral scent replaced airplane smell. He loved the way women smelled. Jack twisted into his seat.

"Flight attendants, please prepare for departure," came the pilot's instruction.

Lizzie bent and rummaged around in her purse for something. Producing nothing, she kicked her purse under the seat, bent her head and cupped her face with her palms.

"Can I help you, Lizzie?" He leaned close.

"Jack?" She drew away from him, her brows furrowed in what he read as disbelief and maybe a pinch of anxiety.

The color drained from her face, and her posture stiffened. "Has something happened to Charlie?"

Charlie didn't tell her he wasn't coming? "Don't worry he's fine."

Jack tried to give her a reassuring smile despite his

confusion. Her distressed expression didn't change, but her shoulders sagged down a couple inches.

"Charlie asked me to stand in for him as your date for this weekend." He reached his right hand in her direction. "Good to see you again."

"My *what*?" She ignored his outstretched hand and stared at him.

A few heads turned in their direction. He withdrew his hand and lowered his voice. "Charlie. Asked me. To come. Remember?"

"Don't patronize me." Her face reddened, and she shot green licks of fire from her emerald eyes that, if possible, would have melted him in the leather seat. "You're *kidding* me, right? Charlie stood me up?"

"Obviously, he didn't tell you."

"Hell no. I'll *kill* him."

Jack huffed. "Not if I get to him first."

Jet engines whined and the acceleration forced him back heavily into the seat with the plane's forward momentum and increasing incline. Through the window buildings shrunk and the wings dipped as they looped over Lake Michigan.

"What am I going to do now?" She bit her thumb cuticle ferociously. "I'll just have to turn around when I get to Boston. I can't go alone. This is…this is just…this is *unacceptable,* that's what this is."

"Hey. Hello. Me plus you does not equal alone. I'm the innocent proxy here. And a damned nice guy, too."

Her hands tightened in white-knuckled fists on her lap. Prepared to deflect one of those fists aimed in his direction, he glanced at her face.

She looked deflated, vulnerable. He liked the green

sparks shooting at him better. A woman that challenged him ignited his fire.

"It's just that I really need Charlie this weekend. I can't believe he could just send somebody else instead."

"Lady, you're doing wonders for my fragile ego." He forced a smile.

Lizzie laughed. "Fragile? I'll bet."

She chewed another cuticle and then skewered him with her gaze, her lips twisted with disdain. "I'm so mad, I'm about to explode. I'm stressed-out enough about this weekend without having to deal with you."

Were women born with the ability to shrink a man down to size with one look? *I have better things to do with a weekend than cater to a moody female.*

"I wouldn't want to add to your *stress*. We'll go separate ways when we get to Boston," Jack asserted.

Plucking the airline magazine from the seatback pouch, Jack opened it, feigning disinterest. *What is going on here? Charlie's motives had seemed clear—a simple favor to a good friend.* Jack couldn't see her with a guy like Prescott. Didn't fit with the impression of her he had through his brother or his own snap judgments, sweet, loyal Lizzie. This feisty woman's rejection brought out the fierce competitor in him while making him feel slightly unworthy.

He reached over the metal console between their seats and seized both of her hands. She flinched and tried to tug her hands out of his, but he held on.

"Listen, Lizzie, Charlie didn't want to disappoint you, but he couldn't face all those strangers. So he asked me to help him. And when I found out it was for you, I agreed because you helped me get him on the right track and back to work. I figured the least I could do for Charlie's sake, and to repay you, is show up, act like the doting boyfriend or whatever it is you have in mind, and make old Wally jealous."

"Old Wally? Did you say make old Wally jealous?" She yanked her hands away. "Exactly how much did Charlie share with you about my personal life?"

Her eyes shot emerald rockets at him now—more than temper there.

"All I know is back at old "U," Wally dumped you and you're still hurting from it. And he'll be at this shindig in Boston, and you're not up for facing him alone."

Outrage flashed over her features, and he thought better than to stoke her anger higher. "All right." He held his arms up in a pose of mock surrender. "Maybe Charlie didn't exactly put it that way. But the way I see it, you shouldn't let Wally have a second chance to hurt you."

"I really don't need your opinions, and, for the record, he detests being called Wally. I'd like you to forget this whole thing." Her lips froze in a tight line and she heaved a sigh.

The soft rise and fall of her breasts beneath the white sweater she wore distracted him. Logic dictated keeping her at arm's length. *Then why do I want to take her in my arms instead and unfreeze those lips?*

"I'm sorry." He put his finger lightly under her chin to tip her head up toward him. "Really. This switch without your knowledge was wrong, and we'll deal with Charlie. But I do want to help you, if you let me. Charlie made it clear how important you are to him. He trusts me enough to take his place. If you give me a chance, I'll be Charlie in every way. Except better looking."

Dislodging his finger from under her chin with a poke of her hand, she squinted at him and scrutinized his face. "I guess I have no choice, now do I?"

"If you put it that way…" He paused, giving her a chance to retract or rephrase her question. When she didn't, "You know women usually are a bit more…enthusiastic about spending time with me."

Dead serious, she tossed out, "You'll do."

Chapter Five

When they entered the baggage claim area at Logan Airport, a limo driver, among a cluster of others, held up a grease-board sign with "Clark and Moran" written on it.

Impatient and uncomfortable with Jack hulking near, Lizzie shifted from foot to foot and waited for the carousel to start. She pointed out her two over-stuffed bags to the driver when the luggage moved under the flap curtain into view. Grunting, the driver swung the bags onto a caddy.

"Is that it, ma'am?"

"For me, yes." Lizzie folded her arms across her chest and watched the driver look at Jack.

"I'm good." He shifted the small duffel bag to his other hand.

"That's *all* you brought for this weekend, Jack?"

She didn't know anything about Charlie's brother. Neither Charlie nor Mari had ever mentioned exactly what Jack did for a living. If they had, she didn't remember. Maybe something about construction work. She hoped Jack had formal wear tucked in that little bag, but doubted it.

"You'll need a tux for Saturday night not to mention a sport coat for this evening."

"I'm good. Don't worry, princess. I won't embarrass you in front of your high class friends."

His mocking tone grated on her nerves making her want to retaliate. Aware of the bulk of Jack, the sense that he towered over her, Lizzie was tempted to berate him for his snotty tone and demonstrate that he couldn't intimidate her with all that brawn. Swiftly her reaction to his nearness changed to a blast of sheer attraction that gathered a sexual pull in her and spread like molten lava. She resisted the urge to fan her face with her hand.

What was with her? He wasn't her type at all. Good to look at, but that's about it. He was too big, too rugged, too sure of himself.

Did he plan to wear jeans and a T-shirt all weekend? She didn't want to create a juicy scene in front of the driver, so she bit off a retort and followed the two men to the car.

The driver stowed the luggage and whisked them toward Cambridge.

Jack didn't invade her space during the quiet drive. She stared out the window as the sun turned the Charles River into an undulating lens that reflected a kaleidoscope of colors. Crews rowed on the river. Students ran along its shore. Families picnicked in the grass.

Strange to be back where she had experienced so many life-altering changes. How many hours had she jogged along those banks thinking about Wallace and her parents?

"Beth, you look a million miles away."

His sudden use of the nickname caught her off guard. Only her dad had ever called her Beth, his loving pet name for his only child was a cherished memory for Lizzie. "Don't call me Beth. My father called me Beth." She didn't mean to sound quite that snippy.

He shrugged. "I'll have to remember that."

"So many memories for me here and not all of them are good ones. I have a few ghosts to deal with this weekend. This is the first time I've come back since…"

She really couldn't talk about it, the pain barely forgotten each day she woke up. *Momma and Dad gone in an instant, Wallace disappearing without explanation after we spent the night together. So hard to be here and not relive the anguish of being so horribly alone.*

And Charlie had abandoned her, too. "I was relying on Charlie to lean on."

Jack sat beside her in the car in silence, and she was grateful he didn't press her to tell him more.

Finally, he interrupted the silence, "These are big shoulders. Lean on them whenever you want. Pretend they belong to Charlie."

Jack's simple offer of friendship to her, a virtual stranger, impressed Lizzie. But she didn't trust that easily.

Still he seems to be a nice enough man who doesn't deserve displaced anger.

"Thanks, Jack. I mean it. Thank you for coming this weekend."

He nodded. "You're welcome."

She still wasn't sure if this arrangement would work, but at least she'd give it a chance. *As if Charlie gave me any other choice.*

The car crawled across the Charles River Bridge, and they entered Harvard Square. Passing bicycles and pedestrians, they pulled up in front of The Charles Hotel.

Before the limo fully stopped under the hotel portico, a uniformed bellman pulled open the rear door of the car and welcomed them. At the lobby desk, they discovered that, as promised, Charlie had taken care of all the arrangements for two prepaid suites. Jack left Lizzie at the door to her room to shower and change for the welcome reception.

Lizzie found a huge arrangement of long-stemmed red roses on one of the antique tables in the sitting area of her room. Expectant, she ripped open the small envelope skewered on a long plastic fork in the vase.

Disappointment twisted her stomach as she skimmed over the message of apology to see Charlie's name at the bottom of the card. What kind of fantasy had she concocted for the weekend? Wallace sent the roses in repentance and he'd beg her to come back to him?

Still mad at Charlie, she threw the card in the wastebasket.

What a stupid idea to be here. How would she get through this alone?

Yes, there's Jack. And yes, he's a distraction from some nervous tension. *But he's so different than teddy bear, Charlie. He unhinges me.* Before she could pinpoint why, the phone rang and she reached around the vase to answer it.

"Hey, Bella. Where are you? I've been trying to get you on your cell phone. Oh, wait. Don't tell me you forgot it again."

Kay's good-natured laughter was the best medicine.

"Yep. I'll have to buy another one if I need mobile communication the next few days. We got here a few minutes ago. We're just changing, and we'll be there as soon as we can. Charlie arranged a car for the weekend, so we don't need a lift."

Wandering to the window, portable phone pressed to her ear, Lizzie fingered the sheer curtains, found the center seam of one panel and moved it aside bringing the vista outside in focus.

"Great. I'm so surprised Charlie came," Kay commented. "I can tell you now that I didn't think he would. I expected him to back out at the last minute."

Despite the number of people engaged in assorted activities down below her, the room was unnaturally quiet as if Lizzie were insulated from the rest of the world.

"What are you psychic? Charlie did bail on me, and I didn't know it until they closed the airplane door." Lizzie dropped the curtain and plopped down on the edge of the bed. "He sent his brother, Jack, instead. Kay, what am I going to do? Have you seen Wallace yet? Can you believe this? How mad will you be if I just head to the airport now?"

"Ah, Lizzie." Kay's breathy voice sounded exhausted. "I guess I won't be fighting mad, but I think you should stick it out. For purely unselfish reasons, sweetie. Confront this, confront Wallace and be done with it."

Lizzie heaved a sigh and closed her eyes. "I don't know why I came in the first place but here I am and with a perfect stranger."

"You came because you love me. We'll have fun. Don't worry so much. What's this Jack like? What does he do? Is he cute?"

Lizzie's cheeks burned. "He's too cocky, very full

of himself. But he's really being sweet to me, which is kind of unbelievable when you consider the circumstances. But so was Wallace, sweet at first, always so sure of himself, and my biggest regret is that I trusted him."

Like a fool.

"I've been wracking my brain trying to remember if Mari or Charlie talked about Jack's occupation. Mari tried her hardest to get us together. I always managed to evade that whole thing. I think he does something in construction with his grandfather. I guess he's cute if you like tall, dark, sculpted men."

"This weekend is shaping up to be very interesting. Go change and come over to the club. We're waiting…all four of us. This fat lady hopes you brought Fannie May in your suitcase with her name on it. Bring it with you. My hormones are begging for chocolate."

****

Jack dressed for the evening after a leisurely shower. A concierge service sent a tux, half a dozen custom shirts, a sport coat, several pairs of slacks and some toiletries to his hotel suite. He had some casual stuff in the duffel.

As directed, he met Beth under the hotel portico. He liked calling her Beth instead of Lizzie. Beth matched how she looked, soft, unique.

The limo came in handy with no available parking around the Varsity Club. Jack entered the packed room, Beth's hand folded loosely around his arm. Conversations buzzed. Two-tone banners of green and white, probably in school colors declared, "Welcome Class of 1997…A Decade Better!"

Yeah this was going to be a big pain in the ass.

Jack had offered to carry the two-pound box of candy for Beth. Her hand trembled when she pushed a strand of chestnut hair behind her ear. He reached out to hold that ice-cold hand to give her support, but she pulled it away and stared straight ahead. He didn't take offense at the brush-off. Chalked it up to nerves. How could this beautiful lady let the likes of Wallace Prescott cause her grief?

Before Jack could get acclimated to the crowd and the noise, a short, stocky man supporting a very pregnant woman on his arm, cornered them.

"Thank God you're finally here. There's the candy!" Both arms of the pregnant woman were outstretched in front her, and her hands opened and closed. "Hand over that box, and no one will get hurt."

Jack surrendered the candy to the grasping woman, surprised that the two-pound box didn't alter her center of gravity and tip her over. He watched, smiling, as Beth threw her arms around the woman, then the blond man hugged both of them tight with his eyes closed.

"Kay, Mick, this is Jack Clark. Jack, Kay and Mickey Lynch. Maybe we should at least try to be civil before you dive in to the chocolate, Kay."

"Hi Jack. Nice to meet you." Kay's head dipped as she tore the box of candy open and tossed the lid on the floor. "Easy for you to say, Liz. You haven't had to sit here for the last hour and deal with these idiots. You wouldn't be civil, either."

Kay bit into a fat chocolate and released an orgasmic sigh.

Jack couldn't remember having such an instant connection with two people. Beth Moran had great taste in friends.

Mick clamped a warm hand on Jack's shoulder. "She doesn't need me when she has chocolate. I think I'll go find a beer. Care to join me, Jack?"

Jack trained his eyes at Beth for her approval. *No need to leave her alone the first five minutes we're here.* She and Kay laughed and released the men with nods of their heads.

Sitting with Mick and a few of his buddies at the bar, Jack observed his "date" accompany Kay over to the name badge table. Beth looked pretty in her demure knit suit, the color of her eyes. He enjoyed watching the way the material clung to her rear end, the short skirt even better than the jeans she wore on the plane. She moved gracefully in very spiked high heels that looked like they hurt like hell, but they didn't seem to bother her.

Her long hair worn down and loose instead of the customary pony tail, lustrous brown curls bounced against her shoulders, an invitation to thread his hands through it.

"What can I get you?"

Jack swiveled on the seat of the bar stool toward the man's voice. The bartender planted his palms on the bar in front of him and Mick.

"Coors for me." Jack turned toward Mick. "Let me spot this round, Mick."

"Sounds good, I'll have the same. We can run a tab and split it."

Jack nodded in agreement, then swiveled back around to take in the action in the room while Mick conversed with the man next to him.

Beth captured his attention again. Jack couldn't tell if she had makeup on, but since her freckles seemed faded, she must have done something to her face. Something captivating. Why was he giving her the once over? He had no interest in the cool slim princess.

He couldn't wait to get his hands on his brother for neglecting to explain why he reneged on his promise to Beth and sent him instead without her permission. No surprise that Charlie didn't pick up the phone when he called him from the hotel. But he wouldn't be able to duck him for long.

The bartender produced the drinks, and Jack reached a hand to grasp the handle of the beer mug. Clinking the glass against Mick's he toasted, "To new friends."

"To friends," then Mick held his mug out in front of him, "new and old."

Jack resumed his role as a spectator. Groups formed, broke apart, reformed as people milled around the room. Beth stood, rounded the name badge table and hugged two women enthusiastically. Jack recognized Wallace Prescott when he walked into the club, even though they'd never met. Clad conservatively in a navy blue blazer and khaki pants, Wally should have blended in with the rest of the men there. But his haughty expression surveying the room smacked of superiority.

Did the snob expect everyone to stand up and clap because he had arrived?

Prescott had what looked like a Victoria Secret model hooked into the crook of his right arm. His mud brown eyes prowled until they landed on Beth chatting in front of the table. Prescott's territorial gaze never left her, while he shook hands and slapped backs as he wound his way in for the strike. What the hell did Beth see in this jerk?

"Excuse me a minute, Mick." Jack rose, watching Beth who now stood alone by Kay's table, her back to the door and Prescott's forward advance.

Jack hastened over to Beth and put his arm around her.

Drawing her against his side, "There's my girl. I missed you." He made sure his tone was plenty loud. Jack brushed a tender kiss across her warm cheek.

*****

What in the world?

Blindsided by the public display, Lizzie leaned left against Jack's rock hard arm and raised a hand to nudge him away.

He deflected the swat of her hand by grasping it and kissing it. Bending his head to her ear he whispered, "Tell me that's not Wally behind us, and I'll let go."

His warm breath on the sensitive skin of her ear causing a heady imbalance, she located Wallace about fifteen feet away facing in her direction. Alarm pierced her at the pending confrontation.

"You're right, that's him," she whispered, her heart racing. He was still handsome and he still looked at her as if he owned her.

Jack's bracing arm tightened around her shoulder. "Thanks," she gave Jack credit for flawless acting, looking up at him with genuine affection. Then she focused on Wallace's face.

Did he look jealous? Good. Nobody deserved it more.

Despite the tiny zestful feeling of having the upper hand, Lizzie quaked inside with gladness seeing him again warring with a tumble of emotions; remembered longing, hurt, dashed dreams and a maddening bite of inadequacy.

Wallace unlatched a showy woman from his arm and strode directly toward her. "Elizabeth. I am so glad you were able to come. I was hoping you would."

He ignored Jack wrapped around her and grabbed her hand, held it a beat, and cast her a wistful smile, then let it go. He shifted his eyes upward toward Jack, a quizzical, defiant expression on his face.

Lizzie's heart hammered, and her breath caught in her throat. She had dreamed of and waited for this moment for so long. She leaned full-tilt against Jack. If he moved, she'd fall on the floor.

"Good to see you too, Wallace." Proud her voice sounded steady and clear even though her insides had turned to Jell-O, she looked up at Jack with a flirty bat of eyelashes. "I want you to meet Jack Clark."

"Hello Jack." She knew Wallace too well to miss his snide and dismissive tone.

"Hi, Wally. Nice to meet you." Jack still held her close and with his free hand pumped Wallace's hand, and then dropped it. "Are you a friend of Beth's? She's never mentioned you."

The invisible glove smacked Wallace's face.

Wallace smiled thinly. "I prefer Wallace, Jack…Clark, is it? Elizabeth and I dated in college, didn't we, Elizabeth?"

She shuddered at his choice of words. Such a paltry description of what she thought they were to each other.

Jack swung his right arm around to circle around her and squeezed. "Beth and I are a bit beyond *dating.*" He grinned at her, blue eyes dancing, and she bit back a laugh.

"I should never have let her go." There was Wallace's wistful smile again aimed straight to her heart.

Lizzie's heart skipped, swelled as if cueing the live band which suddenly opened with Louis Armstrong's *What A Wonderful World*.

Wallace's apparent "date" shouldered her way into the group. Without a word, the tall, anorexic thin woman steered Wallace to the dance floor while he called over his shoulder, "We'll talk later."

Lizzie hadn't moved an inch during the brief exchange and still nestled in the curve of Jack's arm. He leaned down and brushed his lips on the top of her head. She turned her face up to meet his eyes.

"Thank you," she whispered. "Keep it up. I think it's working."

"Want to dance?" He didn't wait for her response, just nudged her onto the dance floor and took her in his arms.

She closed her eyes and let him lead her slowly, soothingly, around the floor. Protected and insulated from the assorted emotions of seeing Wallace again, gradually her pulse steadied.

Wallace was still interested in her. *"I should never have let her go."* And she had never forgotten him, always hoped, while she love-hated him that he would be interested in her again.

But warm and enveloped in Jack's arms, she stopped thinking about Wallace or the past. She didn't think at all, relaxed and moving to the music.

The crowded dance floor left little room for more than swaying. Cocooned in a little pocket toward the center of the pack, Lizzie noticed Wallace and his partner on the outer fringes of the floor. His eyes tracked her, never left her, although she did nothing to acknowledge his attention. She laid her head on Jack's chest and savored the moment.

****

At midnight the band played its last set. Jack trailed behind her as she said her good byes to Kay and Mick after agreeing to meet for breakfast the next day.

"I'll see you in the morning." Jack shook Mick's hand. His eyes softened as he reached for Kay's hand and kissed the back of it tenderly. "Thanks for a nice evening."

"See you tomorrow, Jack." Kay beamed; she obviously liked Lizzie's proxy date.

Jack rounded the car as the driver held the car door open for Lizzie, and she slid into the seat as Jack got in the back on the other side.

"I like Kay and Mickey," he said, his tone soft, relaxed. "I could tell right away that they're good people. Seems like I've known them a long time. I do not, however, like your Wally. I don't understand why you're wasting your time with him. But it's none of my business."

Do I want Wallace back? What do I want? She only knew she didn't want to end this wonderful evening with a disagreement. "I'm glad you were with me tonight. You were the perfect escort. Charlie couldn't have done better. Thank you."

"I'm not sure I like being called an escort," he took his eyes off the road and cast her a bemused smile. "But you're welcome."

"Really, Jack. Thank you for all you did tonight.

You went above and beyond any brotherly promises you made to Charlie."

"No problem. Glad to do it."

Lizzie leaned against the seat, sighed and the tension let loose for the first time since the flight.

Chapter Six

Lizzie awoke at dawn, sleep deprived after a restless night. So tired when she and Jack returned to the hotel from the reception the night before, she'd barely had enough energy to work the lock.

But by the time she washed her face, slipped on a nightshirt and climbed into the luscious king-sized bed, she was too wired to close her eyes.

The events of the evening replayed in her mind, especially the part where Wallace had looked at her with hunger in his eyes. What exactly did that mean? Could there be a chance for them again?

She stayed awake, thought about Wallace and wondered if he loved her. Repeat history. Wallace had caused sleepless nights before, during and after their relationship.

Rolling on her side, she stretched closer to the night table to see the face of the Bose clock radio. Seven A.M. She would much rather have breakfast with her friends alone, but would have to at least call Jack and ask if he still wanted to join them.

Shaking free of the down comforter she padded to the window and pushed the heavy draperies open. Sunshine glinted on the river and people engaged in all kinds of exercises along the banks below her. It seemed like a perfect day for walking. She dialed Jack's room.

He picked up on the fourth ring. "Aah?"

"Good morning, Jack. I'm sorry. Did I wake you?"

"It's okay." He cleared his throat. "Are those numbers right on the clock? Is it 7:03?"

"Yep. It's seven. I shouldn't have called, but I wanted to check in with you before I left to meet Kay and Mick for breakfast. You don't have to go. I'll touch base with you later about the plans for the gala tonight. It's a sunny day so I plan to walk to the restaurant." She spoke fast hoping that she could get the call over with and he would go back to sleep.

"I'll have to take your word for it. My drapes are closed, and it's still as black as midnight in here."

Rustling. "Give me a few minutes to throw on some jeans," his voice was losing some of its morning roughness. "I'll come along. I'm starving."

"Oh, take an hour. I'm not showered yet anyway. See you downstairs at eight?"

"An hour? OK. I can sleep for forty-five more minutes. See you in the lobby at eight."

****

The elevator doors opened at 7:58, and Jack strolled out of the car with a long-limbed, lazy gait. Unshaven, his damp black hair finger-combed away from his face, he wore well-aged blue jeans and a long sleeved Illini sweatshirt.

He cut such an imposing figure that she noticed no one else in the crowd. Towering above everyone, he strode with athletic confidence toward the corner of the lobby where she stood. Her stomach quivered. Why was she nervous?

Powerful thigh muscles flexed under denim and the material of his faded orange sweatshirt pulled taut over his chest. His dark hair curled slightly at the ends to mid-ear. She had an urge to touch it and see if it felt soft or course against her skin.

His beard stubble would surely grate against her face if he were to kiss her. The heat of a guilty blush crept up her throat from the fantasy.

Composing her face into, she hoped, a neutral expression. "Good morning, Jack."

"Mornin', Beth."

She let his repeat use of her dad's nickname go. Couldn't control Jack anyway. And she liked the soft inflection he used when he called her Beth. It somehow made her feel safe, like she had felt when Dad was still alive.

"I thought we'd leave early so we can walk for a while and take advantage of the weather. Want to wander around town a little?" Lizzie cocked her head, waiting for his reply.

"Sounds good to me. I could use some exercise."

Jack held the door open for her and she walked outside. The fall colors had passed their peak. Brown leaves crackled underfoot and lifted in swirls with the breeze. The ancient trees still held most of their crowns of yellow, crimson and ocher.

Lizzie scuffed her feet along the cobblestones and pushed leaves ahead of her. Nostalgic, she looked at the piles of leaves in the street along the curb, wishing she could jump in them. Fall was her favorite season.

Breathing deeply, the crisp clean air renewed and invigorated her. Things were finally falling into place. She couldn't wait to see Wallace again later.

She led Jack to the bridge over the Charles River. Racing shells speared through the water below. Crews moved in unison like an upside down centipede. People stopped along the span of the bridge to watch the boats and turned circles to take pictures from the vantage point of the middle of the river.

****

Beth kept her distance from him, at least a foot was between them the whole time. He listened to her guide-talk as she picked out points of interest. At first he considered telling her he had done graduate work at the university, and he knew every inch of the streets they traveled but decided against it. This was her show, and besides, things looked new to him through her eyes. Funny how he didn't want to control the conversation.

When they arrived at the Greenhouse exactly at nine, Kay and Mick had already snagged a table at the insanely crowded restaurant. Beth guided him past the line that formed out front.

Threading the way toward Beth's friends, Jack didn't interrupt her rambling, "Everybody loves this place. Kids, parents, faculty. Doesn't matter that it's always so packed it's almost claustrophobic."

He knew it well. The menu took fifteen minutes to read, the portions were gigantic, the prices reasonable and the food legendary.

"Hey guys. Thanks for getting the table." She hugged Kay and Mick and then sat.

"We can eat now. Yay," Kay hooted.

Two steaming mugs of coffee waited at the empty places at the table. He followed Lizzie, sat beside her and placed his order with the others.

The waitress returned in minutes balancing their overflowing plates in each hand and on her forearms.

He dove into his fluffy omelet and watched Kay dive into hers with the gleeful avarice of a pregnant woman. Stuffed, he sipped his coffee amid butter and cinnamon aromas, the clatter of metal utensils against plates and the din of overlapping conversations.

"That was some party you threw last night, Kay." Jack leaned back, stretching his legs out under the table with one arm across the back of Beth's chair. "Everyone seemed to enjoy themselves."

"Wait until you see what I have planned for tonight. I have a few surprises up my sleeve that even Lizzie doesn't know about. You went to the University of Illinois?" Kay pointed to his sweatshirt.

"For three years. Then I was out of there and never looked back." He had been determined to finish the normal five-year architecture degree in three years so he could help at the firm due to his grandfather's failing health. That man had meant everything to him, and he missed him every day.

"Well college isn't for everyone," Kay concluded. "Is anyone going to order dessert? I have to have a piece of that mile high chocolate cake."

Kay signaled the waitress and asked for the cake. "I'm not sharing. If you guys want some you have to order your own." She looked pointedly at Mick.

"No takers here." Beth eased back in her chair and groaned. "I'm so stuffed I can't eat another bite."

Jack liked the way Beth smiled as Kay dug into a mound of chocolate butter cream.

"What's planned during the day today, Kay? Can I help you with anything?" Beth leaned her elbow on the table, cupping her chin in her hand.

"The boat ride is at noon, or I should say the boat rides. There are too many people for just one boat, so it'll be more like a flotilla." Kay shook her head. "It was a pain in the ass to get it all arranged. The lunch caterer had conniptions when she heard that her buffet had to be tripled. Thank God, money talked. You bought tickets for you and Jack, right?"

"Sure." Beth swiped her finger through the cake icing and stuck it in her mouth. Her green eyes widened in feigned innocence when Kay held her fork in stab position over her dessert.

"I bought everything the reservation form had on it," Beth stated. "Check-marked every box, wrote the big, fat check and mailed it to the reunion committee care of Kay Lynch. I figured you'd kill me if I didn't."

"You know me so well. And I know you so well that I figure you'll want to kill me when I tell you I don't want to go on the boat ride at all."

Beth grabbed Kay's hands. "Are you all right? Kay has this been too much for you? Do you need a doctor? We can get the car, can't we, Jack?"

Jack extracted his cell phone from his pocket ready to dial.

Kay placed her hand on his forearm, which stopped him from using it. "No, Jack, it's not necessary. Everybody, I'm fine. I just know that if I'm going to be able to stay up past dinner at the gala tonight, I better pace myself and rest this afternoon. That's all." Kay laid her hands on top of her stomach and smiled.

Beth sagged back in her chair. "You scared the life out of me. You want to blow off the football game, too?"

"Yep."

Mickey's face brightened. "Do you play golf, Jack? I might be able to get a tee-time at a course near my house. Maybe we can get in nine holes." Now Mick had his cell phone ready in his hand.

"Sounds good to me, Mick." Jack turned his face toward Beth. "Do you need me to do anything today?"

Beth and Kay grinned at each other and exchanged an unspoken message. "I don't mind if I miss the boat ride or the game," Beth said off-handedly. "I'd rather play golf."

"You play?"

"Not very often. But I have played a few times."

After Mick made a quick call to schedule a tee-time, Jack, Beth at his side, trailed him and Kay the short distance to their car—illegally parked around the corner from the restaurant.

An electronic bleep sounded popping the locks, and Mick opened the door for his wife. "Good. No ticket this time. Kay collects so many of them, parking tickets are one of our monthly budget items."

After dropping Kay off at her house to rest, Mick drove a few miles farther to the course.

Mick had two sets of clubs in the trunk. "You can use Kay's clubs, Liz."

She pulled out several of the clubs inspecting them before hoisting the bag out of the car. "They look brand new. When did Kay take up golf?"

"She had a round of lessons a while ago so she could spend more time with me. She liked driving the golf cart around mostly. Thought it was dumb to make such a big deal out of hitting a little white ball." He chuckled.

Mick grabbed his clubs while Beth stood patient and relaxed in the parking lot, waiting.

Jack shook his head back and forth and pushed his hand through his hair. "Why do I get the feeling I'm about to be hustled?"

Beth fluttered her eyelashes, her eyes wide in phony innocence, as he followed her to the first tee toting his rented clubs from the golf shop.

"Ladies first." Jack swept his arm before him bent at the waist.

Mick nodded and stood beside Jack.

Beth pulled a pair of gloves from one of the bag's pockets, put them on slowly and deliberately, squinted her eyes and gazed at the flag in the first hole, he assumed, gauging the wind. She slid the driver from Kay's bag and stepped to the tee.

"Beth, the ladies tees are up there." Jack pointed. "Dead ahead thirty yards."

"Thanks, Jack. But I'm fine here." She took her time lining up her shot. Jack had a nice view of her rear. Skinny, but not one thing wrong with her ass.

He waited for the first shot of the game with good-humored interest and growing suspicion.

Beth drew the club back in a textbook swing and connected with the ball's sweet spot. A perfect hollow crack sounded, and she shaded her eyes with one hand to track the ball's flight. It sailed in a graceful arc, one hundred and fifty yards at least, before it touched down and rolled on a beeline for the hole. It came to rest almost two hundred yards down the fairway.

Instead of whooping in delight, Beth stood away from the tee and made way for Jack or Mick. She looked as innocent as an altar girl.

Jack belly laughed, impulsively threw his arms around her and swept her in a circle off the ground. "I knew you were a hustler!"

He beamed down at her, his arms locked around

her. She stiffened within his embrace at first, but he didn't let go. With her warm body and the soft press of her breasts against him, he was in no hurry to let her loose. The fresh, sugary scent of her perfume enticed him to bury his nose in her neck. Her sparkling eyes danced with victory, a small, satisfied smile tugged at her full lips, tempting him to taste.

As he stared directly into her green eyes, her body relaxed into the hug, a slight sway toward him, toward more.

"Uh…" She awkwardly pulled back.

Relieved he hadn't been rash enough to kiss her, Jack grabbed a club and kept his mind on golf. "Where did you learn to play?"

"Actually here. When I was in school. I met Wallace September of my freshman year, and he told me that if I ever wanted to see him on weekends I'd learn to play golf. So I did. I took a lot of lessons and I guess I had a knack for the game. When I started beating Wallace, he refused to play with me." Beth huffed a laugh. "Ironic, huh?"

"I would have paid money to see you beat that blowhard. I bet his overblown ego couldn't handle being bested by a girl."

"Don't call Wallace names," she bristled.

He forced a smile. "Sorry," he said, although he wasn't sorry in the least.

Jack glanced over at Mick who winked at him, obviously entertained. "You could have warned me, pal," Jack accused him good-naturedly.

"More fun this way," Mick retorted.

"I'll bet. So…" Jack grabbed a driver out of his bag. "What do you say to a friendly wager, Miss PGA?

What's your handicap?"

"Six."

"Not too shabby. Mine's two. How about I spot you five shots, and what's a bet you can live with?"

"Ha! You only need to spot me four shots. The question is what can you live with? Because you'll be the one paying up. Can your ego handle being bested by a girl?" She dared him with her hand out waiting for him to accept the bet.

"I think I can keep my ego in check." Jack gave her hand a hearty shake. "What are the stakes?"

"How about loser buys dinner back in Chicago? Mick will act as supreme mediator. I always beat him, so he's not betting. Are you, Mick?"

"I know better. Get ready to be taken, Jack, my boy." Mick slapped him on the shoulder.

Jack arched an eyebrow at Mick. "Traitor."

****

Lizzie had never had so much fun playing golf. The easy banter between the three of them helped her relax and be herself. She enjoyed the sight of Jack pushing to win, Mick turned caddy advising him, co-conspirators.

Jack's black hair blew around his face, serious with fierce concentration, and his muscles bunched with every shot he blasted off the tees. He had the advantage of sheer power connecting with the ball, but she had more control.

Lizzie placed her hand over her mouth and tried to stifle a laugh when he missed an easy putt on eight. She smelled victory. Sweet.

Remembering how Wallace wouldn't talk to her for hours the first time she beat him, stopped her from laughing. The fear of how Jack would react when he choked on the ninth hole and she beat him by five strokes held her exuberance in check. She didn't need the four shots he'd spotted her and hadn't thought she would.

"Wow." He scooped up her hand and shook it. "You win. I'm impressed. You're really good. I want a rematch sometime."

Shock temporarily silenced her. He'd congratulated her and hadn't walked off and left her in a huff?

"You would play with me again?" Fear slid down her spine.

"Sure I would. Why wouldn't I? You played a great round. But remind me not to spot you any strokes. Hey, maybe we could play partners and hustle some of my friends." He grinned.

She grinned back, used to a different reaction from men. Well, Wallace. What a contrast.

Jack picked up the golf bag and hoisted its strap over his shoulder. "Let me know when you're free for dinner in Chicago so I can pay up."

"You don't have to buy me dinner."

"I never welsh on bets. You can pick the restaurant."

Lunch at the clubhouse lasted longer than the quick bite they'd intended to grab. A quiet man until he had a beer or two in him to loosen his tongue, Mick entertained Jack with stories of his antics in college, most notably the dogged pursuit of Kay for six months before she relented and dated him. Lizzie had always been part of Kay's inner sanctum so she added Kay's perspective to the anecdotes, and it made for laughs and good-natured ribbing.

Mick dropped them at the hotel when the afternoon sun had swung low toward the horizon. The peach-tinged light softened the day. The landscape surrounding the river looked prettier to Lizzie as it filtered through the pastels of impending sunset. She wanted to linger outside and watch the sky grow fiery as the sunlight extinguished, but she needed to get ready for the gala.

Walking through the lobby next to Jack, her contentment with him at her side surprised her. Close together for the few minutes' elevator ride she almost believed they were a couple.

She slid her key into the slot in her hotel door and turned to him. "We certainly were well matched today, huh Jack?"

"Yes, surprisingly so." His appreciative look flattered her. "I'll come by your room at seven."

Leaning on the doorframe, she watched his progress down the hall, which gave her a nice display of extremely great buns.

He's a good guy. Maybe I won't kill Charlie after all.

Chapter Seven

A hollow knock on her door sounded as she fastened the clasp on the back of a strappy sandal. "Door's open." Bent over, she worked the tiny piece of metal into the hole on the leather strap.

The door hinge creaked. Footsteps echoed on the tile floor, coming nearer. Bent at the waist, Lizzie fiddled with her shoe. The bottom of pant legs, matte black on rich fabric, swung into view.

Jack halted with a half-skid of his mirror-polished black dress loafers, and cleared his throat. "I think I need a defibrillator, Beth. Red is your color. And I like how little there is of that dress."

His thick tone of desire sent chills up her spine.

"Thanks." She straightened, did a little curtsy in place and froze.

Look at you.

Clad in a finely tailored tuxedo, his dark hair slicked back, Jack was the epitome of a dream date. He was classic "black Irish" handsome, narrow straight nose, fair complexion, navy blue eyes that shone with easy confidence. "I could use CPR myself. You look terrific."

"John P. Clark, date extraordinaire, at your service, ma'am." He bowed at the waist.

She walked to a side table and picked up her evening purse, thrilled that Jack would accompany her to her next all-important encounter with Wallace. "Ready?"

He swept his gaze over her from the floor to her eyes. Sensuality simmered behind his even stare. "Nice shoes."

"Manolo Blahniks." She sighed. "It's a vice."

"Well, just keep on sinning." He walked toward her and stretched out his hand. She looked down at the flat, black jewelry box in his palm.

"What's this?"

"Charlie told me to give this to you tonight. Claimed you'd appreciate it more than a corsage. I took the liberty of opening it before I came."

Jack deposited the box in her hand. "I think you'll like it. Go ahead. Open it."

Lizzie opened the box gingerly, conflicted about accepting a present from Charlie through Jack. When she saw the diamond necklace, she couldn't contain her delight. "Oh, Jack. It's beautiful."

He stepped forward and removed the dainty jewelry from the box. "Let me."

Steering her in front of the hall mirror he encircled her neck with the platinum chain. All she could concentrate on was his warm breath on her shoulders. His musky masculine scent scrambled her brain.

Staring in the mirror, she touched the tiny diamond butterfly at her throat with wonder. "Mari wore a necklace just like this all the time."

His eyes met hers in the mirror. "I know. It is Mari's necklace." He stepped away from her.

She turned toward him with a teary smile. Her hand pressed the smooth gold filigree into her neck, stroking the tiny diamond facets under her fingers.

Blinking several times so the tears wouldn't spill, she trained her eyes on his. "Oh, thank you Jack. It's a treasure beyond compare."

Lizzie couldn't define what passed between them, but the power of the moment resonated in her soul. She could hardly breathe. He opened his arms and she stepped into them as if pushed forward by invisible hands. For a few seconds they clung together, fit together.

My dream date. Mari are you here with me?

Releasing her gently Jack said, "Thank Charlie, not me. He must have figured you'd be less likely to bash his head in when you get back if he did something nice like this."

"It's more than nice. It's very special." She took a deep breath. "I don't think I'll ever take it off."

He bent his arm and offered it to her.

****

By the time Jack arrived with his lady in red at the hotel that fronted the Boston Harbor, the open-air cocktail hour was winding down. He got them each drinks before the bar closed and steered her through the sea of round tables, heavy with china and crystal, to find seats next to Kay and Mick, who rose to greet them at table number one.

Jack shook Mick's hand warmly. Next he grasped Kay's hand and pressed it to his lips. "You are the most beautiful pregnant woman in the world."

Kay blushed at his attention. "Mostly belly, that's me."

Jack surveyed the folds of sapphire silk that hung from straps of sparkling jewels. The gown draped her body beautifully and showed off her shapely arms. Her lovely face glowed in the candlelight.

"No, you are not mostly belly. You are one exquisite beauty." He kissed her hand again, and then held the chair next to hers for Beth as Mick held Kay's chair. "Mick, every man in this place is jealous of you tonight." Jack sat down next to Beth.

"Charmer." Kay squeezed Beth's hand. "I've got to get up there in a few minutes, and I'm a nervous wreck."

"Don't worry," Beth soothed her. "Jack's right, you look beautiful."

"I'll have to take your word for it." Kay smoothed a hand over her short blond hair. "And you look sensational, Liz."

At eight sharp the orchestra stopped playing background music.

"There's my cue." Kay pushed out of her chair and walked to the front of the room. She turned on the regulator of a lavaliere microphone clipped to the strap of her gown.

"Welcome Class of 1997. I'm your reunion committee chair, Kay Lynch—back in '97, Katherine Adams."

Kay's yearbook picture appeared on a huge wall screen behind her.

"As you can see," she looked down pointedly at her pregnant shape, "things change in the ten years after graduation."

She smiled. "We are an auspicious group. We are scientists and astronauts. We built buildings and bridges, and served our country in the military and the Peace Corps. We have become husbands and wives and fathers and mothers."

Kay shuffled the cards in her hands. "Some of us lost loved ones on September 11, 2001. Some of us departed earth that day."

Pictures of classmates who died in the Twin Towers rolled on the screen.

"Others died fighting battles in war or against disease."

The collage of photos continued.

"We honor their memories." Kay paused.

"In '97 we dreamed our dreams. Today we celebrate those realized and those we still reach for. Ladies and gentlemen, I present our class, now a decade better."

The lights dimmed and a video played on the wall screen. Kay sat down next to Beth and held her hand. The video ran highlights of their graduation ceremony and the achievements of their classmates.

Then, one by one, Elizabeth Moran's published photographs displayed on screen. A voiceover explained the disturbing images of the world's children orphaned by war, famine, disease, natural disasters and neglect. Her yearbook picture flashed up next and the narrator listed her credentials as a Peace Corps veteran, two-time Pulitzer Prize winner, NewsWorld Magazine associate and member of the International Press.

On to the next classmate in alphabetical order, Prescott soon followed with a blurb on Wallace's successes as an architect.

"Beth, yours is bigger than fathead, Wally's," Jack whispered behind his hand.

Beth gulped water as the video ended to thundering applause, the apparent signal for the wait staff to serve the salad course.

"Are you mad at me, Liz?" Kay's brow pinched together.

"Of course not." Beth patted Kay's hand. "Maybe a little embarrassed. But I am proud of those photos because they changed things for those children. So on second thought, thanks Kay. Somebody here might open their wallet because you did this."

"I, for one, am mighty impressed." Jack picked up the wine glass a waiter had just filled. "Here's to the only Pulitzer Prize winner I've ever known."

Beth swatted Jack's arm as if such an awesome accomplishment were no big deal. "Eat your dinner."

Jack dug into his meal, his mind racing, more than impressed with his dinner date.

****

Kay seemed relaxed and busied herself striking up dinner conversations among the other people at the table, while she nibbled on her own meal.

Lizzie enjoyed the food, and noticed Kay's barely touched plate. She touched her arm. "Shouldn't you be eating?"

"Water gives me heartburn these days," Kay assured her. "Don't worry. I'm taking my vitamins. I demo'd that box of chocolates for lunch." She leaned closer to Lizzie and whispered in her ear. "Wallace at three o'clock."

Lizzie tried to avoid any telltale head movement and glanced to the right. His hair slicked back with glossy gel, resplendent in an Armani tux, Wallace pushed back from his table.

"It looks like he's coming over here." Lizzie swallowed against the clench of nerves.

"Places everybody," Jack muttered as he reached

71

for Lizzie's hand and pressed it to his lips.

Undaunted, Wallace soldiered on and approached their table. He held a checkbook in his hand.

"Good evening, Kay. I enjoyed your presentation. Good job." Wallace gave a smile to the table at large, a smile that didn't quite reach his eyes.

Lizzie knew this unreadable look. It had always prompted guilt in her, a vague sense she had done something wrong and spurred her to apologize. For what? She had never been sure. Jack still held Lizzie's hand, a now familiar stronghold against the barrage of self-deprecating emotions Wallace invoked.

"Elizabeth, you look intoxicating tonight." Wallace ignored Jack. "I was touched by your photos." He waved his checkbook in Lizzie's direction. "I thought perhaps I might make a modest donation to your cause. Would ten thousand dollars make a small difference?"

"Oh." Flustered, Lizzie pried her hand loose from Jack's, linked both her hands together and forced them to be still in her lap. "That's very generous of you, Wallace. I'm overwhelmed."

Wallace angled between Lizzie and Kay and leaned his checkbook on the table. He filled out the check and signed it with an audible flourish. Handing the check to Lizzie, a self-satisfied smile brightened his face. "I left the payee blank for your discernment of the worthiest cause."

"Big word discernment, Wally. Good job," Jack quipped.

Unsteady, Lizzie looked up at Wallace.

Did he know how much this meant to her? Finally he cared about something that was deeply important to her?

Her heart leaped, hopeful. "This is wonderful. I don't know how to thank you."

"Of course." He slipped the checkbook into his jacket's inner pocket.

Wallace stared at her, a soft, pleading expression in his brown eyes. *What does he want from me?*

"Well, then." His tone was as soft as his unspoken plea.

He shuffled his weight back and forth on his feet. "I'll get back to my table. Perhaps you'll save a dance for me?"

"Of course, I will." Touched, Lizzie couldn't believe his behavior. In her past fantasies, he would be generous, giving and he would want her again. Maybe she was dreaming now.

"Better get back to your date, Wally." Jack dismissed him in a monotone.

"I came stag." Wallace bared his teeth in a frozen smile at Jack, excused himself and walked away.

He's alone? Maybe he's not serious about that woman?

The lights on the crystal chandeliers dimmed low, and the banquet hall glowed with flickers of candlelight reflected in a mirrored wall to Lizzie's left intensifying the dream-like nature of the evening so far.

Through the wall of French doors on her right, strings of white lights dotted trees and foliage. The orchestra played something sweet, melodic and heavy on the strings.

"First dance with me, Beth?" Jack pushed his chair back and held out his hand.

She placed her hand in his. Lizzie loved fairy lights and dreamy music. Jack's warm hand covered hers so completely. He pulled her to her feet. She moved, light and graceful, to the dance floor and he took her in his arms.

Resting her head against Jack's chest, the solidity of him, she closed her eyes and let him take her wherever he chose. Grateful for her bodyguard, who fortified her with his strength, she was safe.

When he whispered, "Is tonight going the way you wanted?" His warm breath on her hair sent shivers coursing down her body.

"Yes, so far it's perfect." She looked up at him and savored the special intimacy of the slow dance. His deep blue eyes smoldered with an emotion she couldn't read.

"Wally seems to be coming around," his voice gruff.

"He does seem to be interested in me."

She rested her head against Jack's chest again.

"Want him to make his move?" Jack shifted his hand higher on her back as he turned her in the dance.

"I suppose." Curious about Jack's intentions, she raised her head. His eyes blazed with a fierce and seductive power.

His hand never left her back and pushed her closer to him. Heat pulsed from him, spiking her heartbeat. He bent his head and with one fluid motion tightened his hold even more. His soft lips pressed against hers.

Embarrassed from the public display in the middle of a crowded dance floor, she wanted to pull away. His lips teased, the kiss deepened and the impulse to disengage evaporated. Lizzie didn't care that people swirled near and she didn't hold back. She couldn't. Her lips answered his.

Jack slowly ended the tantalizing connection. He continued dancing; still holding her, but he kept his distance from her body now and looked away from her over her head.

She reeled and throbbed with the reaction he had stirred in her. "Jack…"

"Ssshhhh. Here he comes."

"What?" Her mind didn't seem to be working. "Here who comes?"

"Wally will be cutting in, in three, two…" His voice a low whisper, his breath sent more tingles from her ear down her spine.

Wallace tapped on Jack's shoulder, and he let her go. Jack, straight-faced, stepped away and allowed Wallace to take his place. Lizzie awkwardly linked her hand in Wallace's, so smooth and unlike Jack's, and continued to dance. She didn't feel safe at all anymore.

****

Jack walked off the dance floor back toward the banquet table where Kay sat alone. Her shoes off, she had propped her outstretched legs on a chair.

He sat next to her, took a swig of warm beer from a bottle on the table, leaned back in his seat and watched the dancers.

"Nice kiss out there, Jack." Kay's eyes scanned the dance floor. She sipped some water. "Didn't seem like the lady minded being kissed by a stand-in."

"It worked, didn't it?" Jack shifted, restless in his seat and took another gulp of beer. "Prescott couldn't get over there fast enough."

"True." Kay paused. "Mind taking a little walk with me? I could use some air."

She shifted her legs to the floor with a little grunt.

"I'm not even going to try to put these shoes back on. I hope the stones on the patio aren't too cold."

Jack stood, hand outstretched toward Kay. She clasped it, and he boosted her upright then offered her his arm. She rested her hand in the crook of his elbow as they walked through open French doors to the patio. Outside, she leaned on the guardrail and he sidled next to her, the metal cool underneath his elbows.

Water lapped twenty feet below. She shivered next to him in the bracing breeze off Boston Harbor. He removed his jacket and draped it around her shoulders.

"Thanks, Jack."

He gazed at the harbor lights. The planes landed and took off at Logan airport. The airport water-taxis docked and pushed off the hotel pier. The night hummed, and he tasted sea salt on his lips.

"I introduced Lizzie and Wallace," Kay broke the silence. "I still feel guilty about it.

"I knew him in prep school. Our families hung in the same social circles. You know, Mayflower descendants and all that? Anyway, Wallace was a bit of a heartthrob our freshman year: rich, smart, and good-looking. Lizzie was so thrilled to meet him. She's always been a knockout, so Wallace made out in the deal, too."

"I'd say Wally was the only one who made out on the deal," Jack opined heavy with sarcasm.

Kay's hearty laughter was contagious. "You don't like him at all, do you, Jack?"

He shook his head.

"You're gonna like him even less in a minute." Kay heaved a breath and continued, "Liz fell fast and hard. She never looked at another boy the entire four years they were together. Wish I could say the same for Wallace. But she was oblivious to his tomcatting. Didn't even believe me when I told her. Caused quite a rift between us for a while, actually. During our senior year Lizzie told me that she and Wallace were making wedding plans. She was so excited. The eve of our graduation Liz lost her virginity to him."

Taken aback, Jack turned his head toward Kay and touched her arm. "Kay?"

"I know, I know. I shouldn't be talking about Lizzie's personal life this way, but bear with me okay?" Kay took another deep breath. "She woke up the next morning, and she was alone. She was confused, but so happy about what they'd shared. Figured she'd see him at the graduation ceremony. She didn't...because he was on a plane to Europe."

Jack stood back from the railing and turned to face her. "He just left her flat?"

Kay looked into Jack's eyes. "Yes. I did some sleuthing and we didn't know that until a couple of weeks later, but yes. Last night was the first time she's seen him or spoken to him since graduation eve."

"Excuse me, Kay." Jack turned back toward the banquet hall. "I need to cut back in on Wallace Prescott the Third."

"Wait, Jack, there's more." She tugged him by the hand. "Lizzie has the chronic habit of forgetting her cell phone. Have you noticed that?"

"No," he responded with a headshake.

"Well, she forgot it again this weekend. I don't need a license in psychology to figure out why. The same morning that Wallace left her, she received a call on her cell phone. It was the police from the scene of a car crash. Her parents were both dead at that scene. They were on their way to their only child's graduation ceremony."

"Jesus." Jack leaned hard against the railing and pushed his hand through his hair.

She patted his forearm. "We had an apartment our senior year, and Lizzie stayed there with me that summer. I was getting married to Mick that September, and she didn't want to go home to an empty house in New Jersey. I think she secretly hoped that Wallace would return, and they would pick up where they left off. He returned all right. Two months later. That roughly coincided with the splashy announcement that he was marrying what turned out to be his first and most expensive wife. Lizzie bolted. That's when she joined the Peace Corps."

Jack rubbed his eyes. "Why are you telling me all this, Kay?"

"Because of that kiss I saw you plant on her."

He turned toward her and contemplated her face. Her penetrating, hazel eyes searched his.

"Because I love her, Jack. Because she has never been with anyone else since graduation eve." Her eyes hardened with determination. "Because she kissed you back."

Jack tensed. "You think I'm the knight in shining armor type? Is that what you're asking me to do? Rescue her?"

Kay smiled. "Yeah, I am. Just for tonight. Rescue her from Wallace. He never deserved her."

The simple truth. Jack relaxed. "I repeat. Every man in this room is jealous of Mickey Lynch." He hugged her close. "I've got to go cut in on Wally now."

He didn't need to. When he and Kay returned to the table, Lizzie and Mick were laughing together. Jack didn't see Prescott in the vicinity and didn't ask where he'd gone. Didn't care. Protective, impressed with this accomplished, complicated woman, he couldn't understand how any man could turn his back on her without a word. If Beth wanted to dance the rest of the evening, he'd be the only man to whirl her around the floor.

"Hey, Beth." Jack pulled out a chair for Kay and she plopped down with a satisfied sigh. "Want another drink?"

Beth held up an empty wine goblet. "A glass of merlot, please?"

"Sure. Mick, ready for another beer?"

"I'll come with you," Mick volunteered.

****

"I'm having the best time. I'm so glad I let you talk me into coming to the reunion." Lizzie squeezed Kay's hand, bright-eyed and animated. "Wallace apologized to me, Kay."

"That's good, sweetie." Kay furrowed her brow.

"He explained that he was so young then, so scared by how intense our love was. He felt hemmed in, so he ran away. He claims he's regretted it every day since."

"I'll bet he has."

"He asked if he could call me when he comes to Chicago on business trips."

"Are you going to let him? Honestly, Liz, I thought you would cut Wallace off at the knees at this reunion."

"I gave him my number."

Kay blew out air in frustration.

"Don't worry, Kay. I'm not sure I want to see him

79

again socially. I have to think about it." Lizzie smoothed the skirt of her dress with her hands, a pleased smile curling her lips. "It feels good to be the one who can say yes or no."

****

Jack came back with Mick, drinks in hand, and Beth flashed him a wide smile as she accepted her glass of wine.

The evening wound down and the number of guests dwindled, gone to relieve babysitters, to party at more lively bars or to get out of stiff formal clothes and put their feet up at home.

Jack asked Beth for the last dance, and Mick asked his wife. They danced near each other laughing at Kay's jokes. After the music stopped, Mick shook his hand, and Kay hugged Jack for a long time.

"I'm glad we met, Jack. I hope we'll see each other again some time," Kay professed.

Jack kissed Kay's cheek. "It would be my pleasure. Bye, Mick."

"Take care of yourself, Jack. And our golf hustler."

Beth curled near him in the limo and drifted to sleep minutes after the car pulled away. Jack stared out the window and somehow resisted touching the soft woman beside him while mulling the evening over in his mind.

She's like a sister to Charlie. Hell, that would make her my sister, too.

He'd done a nice woman a favor. Good. She deserved it.

Nothing more going on here. At least for her. This was all about Wally for her.

Damn if that didn't irk him. Wally had taken her

heart and then took off.

Dad, Charlie, Beth.

Jack wagged his head back and forth.

Not me.

She looked groggy as he accompanied her to her door. He took the plastic key card she pulled from her purse and opened the door for her. Turning toward him she stood on her toes, put her arms around his neck and hugged him. Her sweet flowery scent and silky skin drove a spike of desire into his gut.

"Thank you, thank you, thank you, Jack, for everything."

To disengage and tamp down temptation, he removed her arms from around his neck, stepped back from her and held her hands, his arms outstretched. "You're welcome, Beth. I enjoyed it. Sleep well."

"You, too."

He released her hands and strolled down the hall.

Her footsteps thudded behind him. "Jack, wait." He turned around and faced her. "The car will be out front at eight a.m. to take us to the airport. The concierge advised me to leave a little early because of all the construction in the city. I'll see you in the morning."

"I'm sleeping in. My flight doesn't leave until Monday evening. Another reason I agreed to come to Boston this weekend is for a business meeting I had scheduled here for Monday morning."

"Oh. OK." She stood there looking uncertain.

"So, safe flight, Beth. I hope things work out for you and Wally."

****

"Right. Thanks." Suddenly weak, almost sick, Lizzie didn't want to say goodbye. More than grateful, she genuinely enjoyed Jack's company and really enjoyed that kiss. "Uh, have a good business meeting. And…a safe flight back," she said, at a loss to say something more meaningful.

She stepped out of his way and forced out, "Good bye, Jack."

"Bye, Beth. Take care."

She backtracked slowly down the hall. When she reached her door, she turned and watched him walk away, her spirits sinking. "Jack!"

He stopped and faced her. "Yeah."

"Do you think we could get together in Chicago for coffee or something? To thank you for helping me?"

His face lit with a slow grin. "Yeah. That would be nice. And I owe you a dinner. I'll call you when I get back."

"Great. See ya." Lizzie closed the door and leaned against it. She kicked her shoes off into the room and sighed.

Chapter Eight

Lizzie piled freshly folded clothes on the bed. Amused, she watched Marty burrow under the neat stacks and knock them on the floor.

"You monkey." Lizzie scratched the dog behind the ears. "I know you don't want me to go again, but I have to."

She had overworked her little stackable washer and drier by laundering every practical piece of clothing she owned. A three-week stint in Niger involved plenty of packing smarts.

T-shirts and jeans went directly into the open suitcase on the floor. She saved space in her backpack for her cameras. Lizzie hated packing, appreciating the irony that her beloved career involved it so much. She would much rather concentrate on readying her photo equipment than worrying about what she'd wear.

Honored and excited that UNICEF had contacted her about the project, she looked forward to bringing international attention to famished children in crisis. Her heart wrenched at the thought of the suffering due to drought and locust infestations. If she could help the little ones she would do anything, but thousands of children were starving.

Zipping the suitcase closed, she dragged it to the front door and plucked her ringing cell phone off the kitchen counter with her free hand.

"Hello, Elizabeth."

A burst of elation bloomed near her heart when she recognized Wallace's clipped voice.

"Wallace what a nice surprise." She wasn't sure when she gave him her number that he was serious about calling.

"Elizabeth. We didn't have enough time together at the reunion. I have a way to remedy that. I will be in Chicago on business next weekend and would like to take you out to dinner. How does Saturday at seven sound?"

"It sounds perfect, Wallace, but I'm sorry I can't accept the invitation. I won't be in Chicago next weekend."

"Why not? We agreed to see each other."

She frowned at his reprimanding tone. Did he honestly think she'd put her life on hold waiting for him to come to town? "I'm leaving for Africa tomorrow morning. I'll be gone for at least three weeks."

"That is way too long. Well. That is unacceptable."

Of course he expected her to put her life on hold. She always had before when they were together. *Well that was then.* "*Excuse* me?"

"I didn't mean that the way it came out. I was hoping to see you sooner. You are quite the world traveler."

Her pulse slowed some at his much more *acceptable* tone. "Yes, I guess I am. I've traveled a lot in my work. I'm gone more than I'm home lately. I leave for Niger tomorrow morning and have a stopover in Boston. Then I'm gone for the duration."

"A stopover in Boston? How long is your stop over?"

"I have to check my ticket, but if I remember correctly, I'll be at Logan for about four hours arriving around noon. I made plans—"

"Perfect." Her mouth hung open as he cut her off, and still he wouldn't let her get a word in. "Meet me in the baggage claim area. I will take care of everything. I look forward to seeing you again Elizabeth."

She stared at the phone. Did he ask her or did he order her?

"Uh…" The dial tone rang in her ear.

Lizzie hung up the phone and clapped a hand against her forehead. *Are you kidding me?* She couldn't decide if she was more irritated at him for blatantly taking her acceptance for granted or at herself for being eager to see him again despite it all.

Shaking off her ambiguous feelings, she went to her closet. She had to rethink her travel outfit. Loose sweats and a comfortable hoodie wouldn't cut it for a meeting with Wallace. And Kay would give her grief when she cancelled their lunch date.

****

The travel gods smiled on Lizzie the next day. Her plane touched down in Boston and taxied to the gate a full twenty minutes ahead of schedule. Butterflies danced in her stomach as she grabbed her backpack from the overhead compartment. The notion that she and Wallace would be alone for the first time in ten years filled her with trepidation.

Lizzie didn't know him at all. She had changed so much in the years since they had been together. How had he changed? Would they still have anything common? Did they ever have anything in common? Questions preoccupied her as she followed the crowd to baggage claim.

Then, she saw him. He wore dark wash jeans and a white button down shirt, his arms full of yellow roses. Her favorite. He remembered. So extravagant, too. She could only enjoy them for the few hours before her next flight. And he'd bought them for her anyway.

"Elizabeth. Wonderful. You are early." He kissed her cheek.

"Oh, Wallace, how beautiful." She sighed and burrowed her nose in the huge arrangement of flowers, inhaling their sweet aroma. "Thank you for remembering."

Grinning at him, she wished the smile he returned warmed his eyes. Delight at his sentimentality extinguished, replaced by self-doubt. *What am I doing with him?* Her stomach churned and her palms went clammy.

He hugged her, his hands on her backpack, and crushed the flowers between their chests. The awkward embrace ended. He loomed taller in her memory, just average now.

"Come." He turned and walked away.

A shimmer of resentment passed through her at his implied expectation that she would follow, obedient. She double-stepped to keep up.

"We don't have much time and I don't want to waste it here in the airport. How was your flight?" He spoke without turning back to her.

Disoriented and trailing him through the glass automatic doors outside into the choke of bus fumes, she darted in between taxis and airport pick-ups following his back.

He stopped by a sleek, stretch limo with darkened

windows, and she questioned him with a glance.

"I wanted to be able to spend every minute with you so I ordered this car. I didn't want to have to concentrate on driving or finding a parking space."

"Well, that's very nice of you, Wallace. I'm impressed."

He donned a pair of designer sunglasses and swung the car door open for her. "And well you should be."

She almost laughed at his joke, but realized in time that he was serious. Vaguely disappointed, she settled into the back of the car.

"It was fate that you had this layover," he mentioned when they were on their way to whatever destination he had planned.

Fate? Maybe. Originally, she had planned to have a fun lunch and maybe a glass or two of wine with Kay, but she had cancelled after his call. Still a sore point with Kay. Did Lizzie let him virtually demand this meeting without considering her plans because she suspected fate at work?

The car glided to the curb near the bank of the Charles River and stopped. Wallace jumped out and headed behind the car. The driver opened the door for Lizzie.

Wallace took a blanket out of the trunk and draped it over his arm. He grabbed the handle of a huge picnic basket and offered her his free hand. She placed her hand lightly in his, and they walked toward the river. Wanting their linked hands to connect her to the only man she had ever loved, she squeezed his hand harder. No reassuring pressure from him to provide her that elusive bond she thought she'd had with him.

The sun, almost directly overhead in a cloudless

sky, warmed her despite the cool breeze that blew off the water and riffs of chills emanating from this frosty man who seemed intent on controlling, or maybe manipulating their time together.

Wallace shook the plaid flannel blanket and set it down on a level patch of grass. He sat on it, plopped the basket down between his splayed legs and patted the blanket next to him. Good thing she had worn pants, that dress she was thinking about would have been ridiculous about now.

"I hope you are hungry." He pulled containers out of the basket and looked like a boy on Easter morning. He held up a bottle of champagne like he had found the golden egg.

"We're having champagne? What a treat," she said tersely, thinking that at least it might help her fall asleep on the plane later.

"Only the best for you, Elizabeth."

Squelching a nasty retort questioning his definition of *best* treatment where she was concerned, Lizzie sat on the blanket next to him, closed her eyes and turned her face toward the sky. Calm, in utter control now, she heard the muted pop of the cork and the vaporous hiss of effervescent wine. She opened her eyes and accepted the flute of bubbling, pale champagne.

"Should we toast?" He looked at her expectantly.

She nodded, curious about what exactly he'd deem worth toasting.

"To second chances. Cheers."

Lizzie was at a loss for words at his show of being the seemingly eager suitor.

She clinked her glass against his and drank.

Wallace gazed deeply into her eyes and looked

about to speak. But he shook his head instead.

"What?"

"Nothing. Let's eat." He popped a strawberry into his mouth and topped off their champagne.

She helped herself to a flaky croissant and watched him. He was handsome; she had always thought so. A former athlete, his body was still taut and lean. His dark brown eyes were shrewd and penetrating. He wore casual Ralph Lauren clothes but still looked stiff. The cut of his streaked, dark blond hair was stylish, but his hair didn't move in the breeze.

What would he do if she rubbed her hands over his head and messed it all up?

Pulling a plastic container from the basket he removed its cover with a flourish, "*Voila.*"

She peered into the container. "Egg Salad? Oh, Wallace, you didn't."

"I did. It's still the only thing I make."

"I remember. The last time I ate it I spent over twenty-four hours in the ladies room."

He laughed and leaned back on his elbows. "I was hoping you had forgotten. Lesson learned. Do not make egg salad the night ahead unless you put it in the refrigerator. Who knew? My word, I thought I had killed you." He waved his hands in mock surrender.

"There were times that day, that night and even the next day that I wished you had. I can't remember ever being that sick."

"I promise you, this is fresh. I made it this morning."

He had spent his morning making a meal for her. A reprise of a meal that had ended badly in the past. The implied symbolism, second chances, do-overs, hit her.

Leaning nearer Wallace took her hand. "I have never stopped thinking of you, Elizabeth. I was a fool to let you get away."

And I have never stopped thinking about you, either.

She stiffened and yanked her hand away as her heart beat erratic somersaults in her chest. "Get away? You didn't let me get away. You dumped me, Wallace."

His features contorted as if pained. "Look. The past can't be changed. We're together now. Can we just enjoy it?"

Glancing away, she stared at the riverbank. True, the past can't be changed.

"I used to feel lucky to be with you. I gave you my heart…" Tears welled as she faced him.

Bending his head, he cupped his chin with his hand, a pensive pose. When he looked at her again, his eyes were serious, hypnotic with intensity.

"I was so egotistical back then I expected it." He shook his head casting his gaze upward. "I didn't deserve you. I've spent ten years regretting my stupidity."

The vice around her heart loosened. "I don't know what to say, Wallace."

Clasping her hands he pleaded, "You don't have to say anything. Just see me again."

"I'll be away three weeks this trip." She freed her hands and bit a fingernail. "Maybe when I get back we could arrange something."

"Three weeks? Does Jack mind?" He squinted, studying her face.

Jack? Why would Jack care either way if I were

gone three weeks or a year? But. Jack would probably care if his girlfriend were gone for that long.

"He understands how much my work means to me." That much probably wasn't a lie. "It's one of the things he loves about me." She smiled, happy with her embellishment.

"Have you and Jack been together a long time?" He focused on her face, unblinking.

"Not too long."

"Does he know that we are meeting today?"

"Of course I told him. We don't keep secrets from each other."

Enough about Jack.

"How about you and your date at the reunion? I'm sorry…I didn't catch her name. Have you been together long?"

"Bunny."

Lizzie snorted, covered her mouth with her hand. "You're kidding," she finally managed.

"She's very proud that she had it legally changed after she appeared in Playboy the first time."

"Wow. You can't make up that stuff. I would never have picked her as the type of woman you'd bring to the Varsity Club. Did you tell her you were meeting me for a picnic?"

"You got me. Bunny is not my girlfriend. I thought I'd make a good impression on you if I went to the reunion with a beautiful woman. She was strictly for show, if you know what I mean?"

She knew. Did he sense that she and Jack were not really a couple and that she had used him to impress Wallace for show? Was he goading her? Had he seen through her sham? She nibbled at her thumbnail.

"I think I understand," she replied carefully. "I think it's sweet that you tried to impress me at the reunion."

"Where did you and Jack meet?"

Damn, why did I bring up the reunion?

"When I joined the Peace Corps I met Jack's brother, Charlie, and his future sister-in-law, Mari. Mari was like a sister to me. We were very close."

"Were?"

"Yes. Mari died eight months ago. I miss her terribly. I'm still very close with Charlie. He has been inconsolable since her death."

"Sorry for your loss. Was Jack in the Peace Corps with you too?"

She wished he'd drop the subject of Jack. Her face burned from skirting the truth. "No, he wasn't with us."

"What does Jack do for a living?"

"He's in construction." How long could she dodge these questions without owning up that she hardly knew Jack? "Why all these questions about Jack?"

"Just interested in the competition, that's all."

"Look at the time." She displayed her watch to him on a bent wrist. "We better head back to the airport. I can't miss my flight."

Jumping up she brushed the seat of her pants with her hands and then helped him put the containers back in the basket.

Wallace put his arm around her shoulders as they walked back to the car. "I would like to see you again when you get back. I have a new project in Chicago so I plan on spending quite a bit of time there."

"Really? Are you putting up a new building?"

"It's not definite yet, but I am sure that we will win

the bid and be awarded the contract very soon. The bid is for the Global Commerce Building. Have you heard of it?"

"No, I don't think so. Good luck."

"Thank you. I know my competition, and I plan on beating him at quite a few things in the near future."

Antsy during the ride back to Logan, Lizzie mentally replayed their conversation on the picnic blanket, incredulous that he had asked her for a second chance.

When he had asked in her dreams her responses were contradictory—yes, with a fairy tale ending and hell, no, with the sweetness of revenge. Could she have a fairy tale ending with him? If she and Wallace picked up where they had left off, she'd have to tell him the truth about Jack. How could she ever trust Wallace if she weren't trustworthy herself?

But that could wait. She didn't know where she was going with Wallace.

"Here we are, Elizabeth."

The car glided up the airport departures ramp. She lifted her backpack into her lap. Wallace leaned over the wilted roses that separated them on the seat. He touched his lips to hers and put his hand on the back of her neck to press her into the kiss.

Lizzie closed her eyes and tried to go back ten years to the heady sensations his kisses had invoked then. But it was just a kiss.

He released her, and she gazed into his eyes. "Thank you for the picnic. I enjoyed it. It would be nice to see you in Chicago."

"Jack won't object?"

She tensed at the pointed question. "No, of course

not. We're not…exclusive."

"Really?" His sarcastic tone grated. "He seemed quite possessive."

"Uh, well…" The driver opened her door and she made her escape.

She leaned toward him from the curb. "Thanks again, Wallace. Take care."

"Sure. You, too. I'll call you, Elizabeth."

Straightening, she closed the car door. Unable to see him through the tinted glass as the car pulled away, she waved anyway before she turned and walked inside the terminal.

During the next thirty-five hours she could think about seeing him again and second chances.

Chapter Nine

Lizzie opened her eyes and froze. She was displaced and only sure that she was in a different place than yesterday morning.

Her cheek rested on a down pillow. She turned her head and looked out the window that framed a view of the Sears Tower like a postcard. The landmark served as her lighthouse that always let her know she was home safe and secure.

She had returned last night from Niger, where she had spent three weeks photographing her "new babies." Emotionally more than physically exhausted, she had fetched Marty from the neighbors, dumped her suitcase and camera gear by the front door, changed into her comfortable, over-worn flannel pajamas and crawled into the soft king size bed.

Anesthetized by exhaustion for twelve straight hours, she had apparently let the television blast and her bedside lamp glow all night.

Reaching for the remote control on her bed table, she clicked the power off button. Soothing silence. She reached under the covers and rubbed the warm fur ball curled next to her leg.

"Hey, Princess, time to get up."

The dog peeked a sleepy, cockeyed face out of the comforter, yawned hugely, burrowed back under the covers and tunneled to the foot of the bed. Snores like only a Boston terrier could make vibrated the mattress under Lizzie's toes.

"Okay. You have a few extra minutes, but after my shower we're both going to Starbucks." She missed her *venti lattes*.

****

While balancing a tray with two large cups and a bag of pastries, Lizzie unlocked her door. She had so much catching up to do. The message light on her answering machine flashed, but she was too tired to deal with it last night.

The machine had arrived a few days after her weekend in Boston. Her managing editor had enclosed a handwritten note:

"Good News! Here's a present for you with my compliments...because my calls are so important. Bonus—this machine stays put so it can never be forgotten."

The note included dial-in instructions to collect messages from outside phones. The instructions were typed on a handy, laminated pocket card. She laughed at the effort her employer had gone through.

Lizzie hit the playback button on the machine. A computer-weird male voice announced she had twenty messages.

Wow, guess I do need this thing.

While she listened to the messages, she divided a mound of mail into piles of bills, catalogs she might look through, catalogs she would never look through, magazines and just plain junk.

Hello, Elizabeth. This is Wallace. I wanted to let you know how wonderful it was seeing you. I'll be in town this weekend and I want to see you again. Call me.

Lizzie's heart thudded in her chest until she heard the phone click on the recording.

She looked at the machine, "Call you? I would, but you didn't leave your phone number."

Hey, Liz. Charlie here. I don't know when you're getting home. Hope you had a successful trip. Call me. Would love to hear all about it. Got the galleys for the book. You're going to love them. Welcome home. Coffee's on me. Love you.

She smiled hearing the strength in Charlie's voice.

Liz, call me. The prints are to die for. Fabulous. Perfect. Call me. If you do, I'll know you're using this machine properly. Your loving editor with more work for you.

Pausing her sorting, she laughed. "Ha," she said to the machine, "I think I'll make you wait until Monday."

Bella. Bella. Bella. I miss you. I need you. I need a party. Who am I kidding I need more Fannie May!!! Call me. Hey when did you get this answer machine? Great idea.

She wrote *order more candy for Kay* on a pad by the phone. Assorted hang-ups and sales pitches had her pushing the delete button as she continued sorting through the mail.

Stretching her bony arms above her head, her recent weight loss was apparent. She hadn't eaten much the past three weeks surrounded by hunger, choosing to give her food away instead.

Elizabeth. Wallace again. I was surprised when you did not return my call. I would really like to get together. Call me.

"Two calls? Wow. I would call if you would leave

your damn number, Wallace." Was he always this frustrating?

Hi, Beth. It's Jack. Jack Clark. Are you free this weekend so I can settle our bet? Maybe we could grab a pizza or something more elaborate if that's your choice. If you're interested please call me. My cell is 312-555-9298 or you can try to catch me home at 312-555-6732. Good night.

Happy at the sound of Jack's voice, she rewound the tape and played the message again. She checked the machine for the date of the call. *What day is today anyway?*

Referring to her wall calendar, she delighted at the picture of Miss November. Marty google-eyed and seeming to smile, was the pin-up of the month. Surrounded by little stuffed turkeys, the dog wore a pilgrim hat. Lizzie had dressed the pup month appropriate, treats at the ready to bribe her to pose, and made a calendar out of the twelve shots. She gave them to everybody she knew as gifts last Christmas to the amusement of her friends. The dog would do anything for cashew nuts.

"Okay. He called Monday," Lizzie figured. So he means this weekend.

"Yes, I would be interested, Mr. Clark. Very interested, as a matter of fact." Feeling jittery, she punched in his home phone number. She almost hoped he wasn't there, so she wouldn't have to be this brave. He answered on the second ring.

She swallowed. "Hi Jack. It's Lizzie Moran."

"Well, hi Beth. Great to hear from you. How was the trip? Charlie told me you were on assignment."

He was talking about me with Charlie.

"I'm so glad I got this assignment, Jack. You can't imagine the horror there. I took shot after heart wrenching shot. I pray these pictures bring attention to the situation. I know where my donation money is going for a good, long time."

"Mine, too. Just tell me where to send checks."

"Thank you so much, Jack. But, I didn't call you to solicit donations. I just got your message and was wondering if you're free tomorrow. I know it's last minute."

"I'm free. I was just going to watch the Bears game with Charlie, but I can TiVo it and catch a game with him next weekend." The warmth in his deep voice encouraged her.

She grinned, pleased with her plan. "Great, come to my place around four. I'll make dinner."

Her words ran together fueled by nerves. She wasn't used to asking a man out to dinner. In fact, she couldn't remember ever asking a man to dinner.

"Are you sure you want to cook? We can go out instead."

"I'm sure. I would much rather eat in tomorrow. I'm a good cook. You'll see."

"I have a cast iron stomach, so bring it on." He chuckled, a deep bass, utterly male sound that thrilled her, making her tingle with anticipation.

"It's a date. See you tomorrow at four, Jack."

"By the way, what's your address?"

She gave him the information, hung up the phone and flew into action.

****

A quick stop at the store after church on Sunday provided Lizzie with fresh, flaky rolls for sandwiches, still warm from the bakery's oven. Their fragrance filled her home and made her stomach growl.

She covered the round, glass dining room table with a green and gold tablecloth. Scooping her famous pepperoni pasta salad into her favorite football-shaped glass bowl, not exactly Waterford, but she deemed it perfect to fit in with her dinner theme.

Heaping dishes of food were on the table, homemade potato salad, rare roast beef for sandwiches, a basil cheesecake dip surrounded by thin crackers for spreading, a spinach dip with peppers and carrots skirting it, and brats with sauerkraut.

To round off the dinner, she'd made her rival Mrs. Field's chocolate chip cookies, and her secret recipe, double chocolate-chunk brownies. She also stocked the fridge with ice-cold beer.

The phone rang, and she checked the clock.

Perfect, he's here. Ten minutes…

Who's on duty at the security desk? She picked up the phone as the answer occurred to her, "Hi Darla. You can send him up."

"Send whom up?"

A droll Boston accent replied instead of Darla's lyrical Hispanic cadence.

"Wallace. Sorry. I thought it was someone else."

"Hello, Elizabeth. How are you? I'm a little disappointed that you did not return any of my phone calls."

The disapproval in his voice made her defensive. "I was out of the country, Wallace, and you neglected to leave your phone number both times."

"Kay has my phone number, Elizabeth, from the reunion. You could have called her to get the number."

He had a way of making her feel like a chastised child. She had forgotten how many times he had talked down to her.

"You're right, Wallace. I could have called Kay. But I didn't."

Annoyed, she let the statement hang. She checked the clock.

Eight minutes.

"Well, what's done is done." He sniffed. "The reason I called was to let you know that I am going to be in Chicago on business next weekend, and I would like you to accompany me to the symphony and dinner Saturday night."

"Sure. Sounds good."

Seven minutes.

"I hate to cut you short, Wallace, but I have to go. Can I call you tomorrow?"

"Yes." He huffed into the phone and hung up without giving her his number.

She put the phone down and it rang again.

"Hello. Thanks, Darla. Yes, I'm expecting him. Please send him up."

The knock on the door brought a frisky Marty on the run from a sunset-colored spot by the window. She stood by the door, wagging her whole body, and waited for Lizzie to open it.

"Hi, Jack. Come on in. Be careful of my watchdog. As you can see, she's vicious."

The pup collapsed, sprawled on her back and exposed her belly, begging him to pet her.

He squatted and obliged. "Fair warning. I have this effect on most women."

"Very funny." Lizzie laughed anyway.

He wore a black leather bomber jacket open over a gray, cashmere turtleneck sweater tucked into ebony slacks and smelled like a walk through the woods. Marty had the right idea. If Lizzie stood next to him much longer, she might want to be petted, too.

Two minutes.

Standing up he handed Lizzie a bouquet of pastel tulips, so exotic this time of the year when spring flowers were a faraway memory. He also handed her a bottle of wine. Her favorite merlot. He took off his jacket and reached into her closet for a hanger.

"Thank you so much, Jack."

This is going to be fun.

Setting the wine bottle on the counter, she tucked the bouquet under her armpit, quickly searched in a cabinet and drew out a vase. She filled it with water, plopped the flowers in it still wrapped in cellophane, set the vase down next to the wine and kept one eye trained on the flat screen TV.

One minute.

Grabbing two beers out of the fridge, she handed him one and grasped his free hand to pull him in front of the TV just as the Green Bay Packers took the field.

Perfect timing.

****

Beth dropped his hand, "Can you hold this a minute?" He caught the beer can she tossed his way.

She unzipped the short gray hoodie she wore with her jeans, draped it on a chair and revealed a torso hugging, Green Bay Packers T-shirt underneath.

"Go Favre!" She bellowed.

Marty froze as if skewered by a lightning bolt, turned tail and ran. Jack's gaze darted around the room, a beer can in each fist. The table bulged with super bowl party food. Beth made a football shirt look like everyman's fantasy. And everyman's fantasy of a flat screen TV featured the Bears/Packers game. "You like football?"

"Like it? I live for it."

"First golf, now football. I think I'll have to marry the girl...of course, only after she changes out of that sorry shirt and puts on the blue and orange of a real team. I'll watch."

"Get real. That's not going to happen. I bleed green and gold."

"Ugh." He grimaced, but he chuckled with the next breath. "Watch your green and gold bleed on the field."

"We'll see." Beth perched on the edge of a leather chair, bratty amusement in her pretty green eyes. Hard to believe he'd enjoy watching a game with the sworn enemy of a Bears fan.

"Where did the pup go?" Jack picked up a carrot. He swirled it in the spinach dip, brought it to his mouth and dripped creamy dressing in his cupped hand. "Mmmmm. Very good."

"Marty hates football. I'm the reason. I've been known to say a few mild words at the TV during the game. Scares the daylights out of her."

As if on cue, the ball slipped through the receiver's hands, and she gave him a demonstration by screaming, "Catch the damn ball!"

"I'm with the dog," Jack quipped.

"Anyway, the minute she hears the game start, she's gone," Beth went on in a normal voice as if the outburst never happened. "I think she has nightmares involving Hank Williams, Jr. on Monday nights."

He arched an eyebrow, "Well, darlin'. The Bears are going to ruin your day and give you nightmares." He grabbed a chocolate chip cookie.

Her Cheshire cat grin back at him made his eyebrow arch higher.

"We will see. We will see," she predicted. "Would you care to place a little friendly wager?"

"You're on. You can't hustle me in the NFL. What's at stake?"

"Loser, by the way that will be you, buys dinner at Malnati's?"

"Best pizza in the city."

"Best pizza in the country. Don't let New York tell you different. Is it a bet?" She had her hand outstretched waiting for his decision.

"Deal." He grabbed her hand and shook vigorously.

The first half passed, Beth on the edge of her seat for most of it, cheering. Jack sat back on a comfortable leather sofa absorbed in the game. He relaxed while she hooted and hollered at his side.

"Half time. Let's eat." She padded toward the table, her bare feet and red toe nail polish sensual, at odds with her all-American outfit. She handed him an oversized dinner plate, and the city lights beyond the curved floor to ceiling windows behind her haloed her body with a fluorescent glow.

"Nice apartment." He took in the spectacular view through a bank of plate glass windows that curved around one width and length of the living/dining area in front of him.

Jack surveyed the spread on the *Green Bay* tablecloth. "This looks great. Where did you get all this food?"

A casual shrug of her shoulders. "I made it."

"No, really, who catered it for you?"

"I'm not kidding. I made it all. Mick was the captain of the football team senior year, and Kay and I would put together a tailgate every week to feed the team and fans after the game. I had lots of practice. We had to get part-time jobs to afford the groceries."

"This is amazing." And this woman made him very hungry.

"Thanks. I hope you like everything."

After filling their plates, he followed her back to the chairs. A comfortable silence punctuated by dog snores from the next room surrounded them as they ate.

"Everything was delicious. I'm stuffed." Jack put his empty plate down on the coffee table. "Here you are in Bears country, and you root for their rivals. Do you have a death wish?"

"I've been a Packer backer it seems like my whole life. When I was a little girl, my dad and I watched sports together. Every Sunday we made elaborate sandwiches and stayed glued to the TV. We watched every sports show we could find. My mom appreciated the day off. She spent the day doing her nails and eating chocolates while she watched her own personal TV in their bedroom. She hated sports.

"One year the Packers were in the Super Bowl. My dad asked if I wanted to make a bet on the game. We shook hands on one dollar. It was an awful lot of money to me. When my Packers won, it was so special for me. I realized, as I grew older that it wasn't because I won the bet, but because my dad made me feel special. Strange, but it was the one and only time we bet on a game. We still watched sports anytime we were together."

Tears gathered in her eyes, and she shook her head. He reached over and held her hand.

"I'm sorry." Beth swiped at her eyes. "It's just that my Dad died suddenly in an accident."

"I know." He gently stroked the back of her wrist. "Kay told me about your parents." Having been through a similar loss, Jack could empathize.

"Oh." The pain in her eyes swamped him. He could only imagine the devastation of losing both parents in an instant.

Then the teams ran back on the field. Beth jumped to her feet and pulled her hand free. "Go Favre!" Past sorrows apparently set aside for football fan mania.

He cracked up. "You're adorable. I could… Go Bears!"

The game ended, and an embarrassed Bears team went back to their locker room.

Jack shook his head, disgusted. "Duh Bears. Here, let me help put the food away."

"Wow, there's so much left. I only know how to make this stuff for an army. Please say you'll take some home with you."

"I live alone and I can't cook worth a damn—so, yes thank you."

He carried dishes into the kitchen. "How about next Saturday we go to Malnati's so I can pay off at least one of my debts? I still owe you a dinner after you skinned me on the golf course."

"I would love to, but I'm pretty sure I'm busy Saturday evening. Wallace called right before you came and invited me to dinner and the symphony."

"Wally? Here in Chicago?" He couldn't keep the edge out of his voice.

"Yes." She turned on the water, squirted some dish detergent in the sink. "He's coming to Chicago next week on a business trip."

Right. The Global Commerce Building presentation is on Friday. Dream on, Wally. That's my baby.

"No problem." Jack managed to speak in a light tone. "I'll take a rain check."

Back off. It's Prescott she's after.

"I'm free the weekend after that." She widened her pretty green eyes in invitation.

Too bad, Prescott.

"Good. Okay." He opened the closet door and pulled out his jacket. "The Saturday before Thanksgiving then. Lou Malnati's on Wells Street. I pay. Pick you up at say, six o'clock?"

"Yep. Sounds good."

She stood near him in the hallway as he shrugged into his coat, in her tight shirt, her hair tousled, her sparkling eyes enticing him.

"Thanks for the dinner. And the inventive refereeing." Her hand brushed his with silken electricity as she gave him the bag of leftovers, and the sweet fragrance of her perfume made him consider burying his nose in the tender skin of her neck.

What am I thinking?

A virtual innocent and a *cheese-head* for godsake.

But Jack had never *enjoyed* a Bears defeat by the Packers, until now.

She moved closer to him, close enough for a kiss, if he wanted to take it.

Smoky flecks shimmered in her jade eyes. Jack drew her close with his free arm and took what he saw offered there intending to kiss any thought of Wally right out of her.

Unrestrained, his lips devoured hers. Jack wanted to mark her, wanted to banish her thoughts of any man except him. Instead he felt himself slip, change. It disturbed and confused him. Still he pressed deeper, wanting more, wanting her.

****

A kiss was never so consuming, a wildfire inside her. Lizzie fused her lips to his hungrily, melted in his arms, her breasts flattened against Jack's chest. Wrapping her arms around him, her fingers lightly traced the ridged muscles in his back, thrilling at the contours.

Stunned by the encompassing power he had over all her senses as his heat collided with hers, Lizzie pressed her hips against him, aching with desire. His arousal pressed at her center spurring an elevator rise of elation and an upsurge of sexual need so acute her arms and legs trembled.

Just when she thought there'd be nowhere else for them to go but the floor, ripping off clothes, his lips left hers, his arms loosened, and the embrace was broken. Shaking and dizzy, she blinked her eyes and stared at him in a stupor, separated from him by inches. Seemingly frozen to the spot, her arms hung at her sides.

His jaw rigid, Jack regarded her with magnetizing intensity. Passion swirled in his night sky eyes. For her. Jack wanted her. Not as a stand-in for his brother. There was nothing remotely brotherly about that kiss.

He made a move toward the door. She brushed her hand on his arm and invited, "You don't have to go."

Hesitating briefly, still staring at her with a dangerous glint in his eyes, "I think I'd better," he said, his voice a low rumble.

He strode toward the door and opened it. Turning his head, unsmiling, he said, "This was nice, thank you." His gaze penetrating, he challenged her. "See if you have as nice a time with *Wally.*"

Facing the open door, Jack tossed out, "I'll see you in a couple of weeks."

He left, closing the door with a quick tug behind him.

Lizzie leaned her back against the metal door. The buildings' lights were a blur through her windows. She rubbed her fingertips over tingling lips, still warm from the surprising, steamy kiss. Jack was a surprising man, and that's not all. Jack was jealous. No other way to interpret that parting jab at *"Wally."*

Comparing men in her life to Wallace had been Lizzie's habit and had impeded her from developing anything more than fleeting relationships in the past. Wallace had never kissed her like Jack.

She did a little end zone dance over to her kitchen sink.

"Are you ready for some football?" she sang out. Then she tackled her dirty dishes.

Chapter Ten

"Yes, Allie." Charlie answered the intercom buzzer.

"Lizzie Moran is here to see you."

Charlie stood and leaned over the microphone on the console. "Great. Show her into the conference room, will you please? I'll be right there."

Unusual for Lizzie to be a half hour late, at least she had showed up. Jack, who was usually very punctual, too, hadn't shown at all.

Charlie dialed Jack's office and found that he was still involved in a presentation behind closed doors. When Charlie scheduled the meeting, Jack had warned him that he might not be able to break away.

Exasperated, Charlie grabbed his coffee mug and headed to the conference room.

He moved down the narrow hallway. *Give me a break will you, Mari? How am I going to bring them together if I can't even get them in the same room at the same time?*

He caught a glimpse of Lizzie through the glass wall. She was bent over the proofs that he had lined around the conference table earlier.

Still frustrated, he swung the heavy glass door open and stepped inside.

She raised her head and banished his sullen mood with her smile. "Hi, Charlie."

He had missed her contagious sweetness. Glad to see her, he forgot his futile attempts at matchmaking.

Setting his mug on the table, he grabbed both her hands and appraised her slim figure in her dark business pants suit.

"You are a sight for sore eyes," he declared. "How have you been? Have you lost more weight? You're disappearing."

"Hardly." She laughed. "But I could say the same for you."

Her brow furrowed. "Are you eating?"

"Yeah, I eat." Slipping his hands from hers, he picked up his mug and gulped.

"Mostly, I drink coffee." He shrugged. "What do you think of the proofs?"

"They're gorgeous." She wandered around the conference table. "I don't know why I waited so long to work with you on a book. I almost don't believe I took these pictures. It's like a dream for me to see them in this form."

"I know. I'm very proud of this book. Both for your artistry and the artistry of the buildings themselves." Charlie picked up a thick sheaf of papers and took a seat at the table.

"I have some paper samples we might use for final printing here, Liz. Want to give me your opinion about them?"

"Sure." Sitting across from him, she sorted through the samples several times and picked out three favorites.

"Thanks." Charlie piled her choices and the rest of the samples separately in front of him on the table. "So how did the reunion go?"

"The reunion? Wow. I can't believe I haven't seen you since then. Maybe that's a good thing since my first inclination was to murder you after you sent Jack instead." She leaned back against her chair.

"I figured as much. But at least Jack was willing to help me, and you weren't let down completely. He seemed to think he did all right by you. Was he right?"

Charlie had talked to Jack when he came back. Something seemed to change with him. Jack wouldn't comment further except to say things went well, but he had seemed guarded, too eager to change the subject. Charlie suspected something had happened, but he might never know unless Lizzie was more forthcoming.

"Yes. It was fun. He was a perfect gentleman. Wallace paid attention big time. I've seen Wallace once since then, and we have a date for dinner and the symphony tomorrow night."

Mari, for crying out loud. A little help here, please?

"That's good." Charlie considered tying her to a chair until Jack made an appearance.

He wanted to see them together and try to figure out what he had to work with to fulfill Mari's wishes

"So Wallace is interested in you again?" *Wallace is an ass and she deserves to be happy.*

"It seems so." Lizzie stood and poured coffee from a pot on the credenza into a Styrofoam cup. "Wallace bought me roses and champagne. He took me on a picnic by the Charles River. It was a perfect day."

Charlie's spirits sank. How could she fall for this guy again? He rubbed his hand through his hair in frustration.

"Hey, did Jack tell you I beat him at golf?" Her

eyes gleamed as she turned around to face him leaning against the credenza. "What a good sport. I had the *most* fun playing that round."

"Why no. He didn't mention that." His spirits lifted some. So Jack was withholding information as he had suspected. "But I'm sure I know why. I don't think Jack would brag about letting a girl beat him on the links."

"Not just any girl. Why don't you come out with me sometime and see if you can beat me?"

Her hopeful look melted his heart. She'd never stop trying to nudge him toward a "normal" life. As if that were possible without Mari.

But he appreciated that Lizzie didn't give up on him. And he wouldn't give up on her, either. She didn't belong with Wallace. Mari had known it and so did he. At that moment, he made up his mind to make sure that didn't happen.

"It's none of my business, Liz, but I got the impression from Mari that Wallace mistreated you. Why are you allowing that again?"

"Hmmm. You know, I always thought that if he were interested in me again I'd feel vindicated. And I could choose him or reject him. I certainly won't accept any mistreatment that's for sure." She drained her coffee cup. "Do you need anything else from me, Charlie? I've got a dinner meeting on the north side with my editor. She's in town overnight, and it's a bit of a command performance."

"No. I guess we're done. I'll get Jack's opinion later. He still might get over here if his meeting's finished. You want to wait a while longer?"

Lizzie looked confused. "No, I can't. Why would Jack have an opinion?"

Charlie laughed. "He probably won't. But I like to run these things by him."

"OK. Sure, Charlie. Well, tell Jack hello for me."

She turned to go, then pivoted back around. "Want to join me and Ellen for dinner? There may be some boring trade talk, but she's a really nice person. It might be fun to get out."

"No, thanks. I'd be outnumbered. Hey, maybe Jack would want to go. You know, even out the genders a little? Let me give him another call." He had to stop this Wallace thing.

Charlie picked up the phone and dialed before Lizzie could protest. Disappointed that Jack was still in his meeting and couldn't be disturbed, he hung up shaking his head and rolling his eyes.

"Guess not." Now he appreciated how frustrated Mari was with the whole matchmaking quest.

She looked at him quizzically. "Charlie, are you all right?"

He tried to brighten the expression on his face and hoped he had succeeded. "Of course. Enjoy your evening, Lizzie. Come on. I'll walk you to the door."

Offering her his arm, he ushered her to the reception area.

Chapter Eleven

"What is your name?" Wallace demanded an answer, peering at the security guard's name badge. "Byron, is it?"

"Yes, sir."

"Well, Byron, Miss Moran is expecting me, and I expect you to give me her floor number right now."

Wallace faced off with Byron. "No sir. You may not go upstairs without a resident escort. You will sign this book and show me a picture ID."

Byron folded his arms, resting his huge hands over bulging biceps and leaned forward, looming toward Wallace. He stared at him, pursed his lips into a solid straight line and waited, stoic and duty bound.

The nerve of this man. As if I presented a security risk.

Wallace pulled a slim wallet from the inner pocket of his impeccable Armani suit jacket, opened it and pried out his driver's license. He slapped it on the console between them with a snap. The billfold probably cost more than one week of Byron's salary.

Byron picked up the ID and read it ridiculously slowly while Wallace fumed. Byron handed it back to him, a neutral expression on his face. "Mr. Prescott. If you'd be so kind as to sign here."

Sliding the visitors' log toward him, Byron placed the tip of a finger on the next blank line. The pressure of the security man's hand on the book was obviously a power play.

Let this underling play his games. I'll figure out a way to get him fired.

Wallace ignored the ballpoint on the counter next to the log and pulled a fountain pen from his inner pocket. He unscrewed its cap and scribbled something indecipherable on the line. May have been his name, maybe not.

He looked up at Byron annoyed with this pointless inconvenience. "What is Elizabeth's unit number?" Wallace walked over and had his hand on the door leading to the bank of elevators.

Byron had the phone to his ear. "I'm calling Ms. Moran right now to tell her you're waiting for her to escort you from the lobby."

Wallace switched direction, "Tell her I'll be in the car." He skirted the security desk bound for the revolving door.

"Asshole," Byron muttered.

Wallace spun on him. "*What* did you just *say?*"

"I said, as you wish." Byron glared at him deadpan.

Disgusted, Wallace shoved through the revolving door outside.

****

Lizzie peered inside the car. "Hello, Wallace. It's so good to see you again."

She took a seat where he patted his hand. The silent driver eased the door shut, walked around the car and took the wheel.

Classical music and Wallace's citrus cologne filled the car. The smells of masculine power enveloped her, Ralph Lauren and luxury leather. He took her hand and held it limp in his.

"It's good to see you, too, Elizabeth. Four weeks was too long. You look lovely tonight."

"Thank you."

"You look perfect for what I have planned this evening." He gestured to the driver to turn at the light. "Much less provocative than the dress you wore at the gala."

Lizzie remembered Jack's reaction to the red dress. She preferred provocative.

"So," Wallace's voice cut through, "we have a great deal to catch up on."

Lizzie looked out the window at the display of Christmas lights on tree-lined streets and building facades and then turned toward him, his features at once in shadow, and then spotlighted by the movement of the car. "It's hard to know where to begin."

"I'd like to begin with the present." Wallace crossed his leg and didn't seem to notice that he'd brushed the bottom of his shoe on Lizzie's silk hose. Miffed, she brushed away a smudge of dirt.

His expression mild, he obviously wasn't taking any accountability. "I've had a very successful series of meetings in Chicago. I'm confident that my design for the new Global Commerce Building will win the day. I'm sure I impressed the panel. First I told them…"

Her mind registered a drone. The car merged into Michigan Avenue traffic, traveled several blocks, and stopped in front of Orchestra Hall. The driver opened the door for Wallace on the street side. When Wallace didn't make a move to open the door for her, the driver raced around the car and yanked Lizzie's door open.

Wallace waited for her on the sidewalk. He placed

his hand on her back and ushered her through gilt framed doors into the vestibule of the great Hall. Then he directed her to a small elevator off the lobby that took them above the concert area to a private dining room.

A few tables flanked a bank of windows overlooking Michigan Avenue. A wood fire flickered in the hearth of an ornately carved fireplace at the far end of the room. Diners conversed quietly and ignored newcomers.

The young Barbie doll hostess greeted them and checked a list on an antique desk at the entrance when Wallace pronounced his name. Lizzie followed the bouncy blond to a table set for two in the center of the room, and Barbie pulled out a chair for Lizzie. She bent to take her seat, but Wallace walked away from the table.

He pointed to a vacant table for four at the window. "We'd like that one."

The hostess's gaze darted back and forth between the two tables. "Sir, that table is reserved for a party of four."

Wallace took a seat at the window table and gestured to Lizzie to come over. "This will be fine. A waiter can remove the extra settings."

Poised over the chair, Lizzie looked at the hostess for direction.

"That will be fine, madam." The hostess clipped every word.

Embarrassed, Lizzie sat down at Wallace's table.

The hostess handed them each a menu and removed two settings. "As you wish, sir." She walked away.

A waiter bustled over and swept a napkin into Lizzie's lap. "Wallace, I don't want to sit here."

"Well, we are." He took the menu out of her hand and placed it on top of his on the table. "So, Elizabeth, I've been rambling the whole way over here. Tell me about your experiences in the Peace Corps. That must have been interesting."

Lizzie had faced a lot of difficulties in her life. The Peace Corps had saved her. And the man who asked her about it, the only man she had ever loved, was the reason she had needed saving in the first place. Surprised, she could think back now, even with him, and not buckle with despair.

"It was transforming. It gave me just about everything worth having. I wouldn't have my career in photography without the Corps."

"But you never used your engineering degree. What a waste."

He plucked a roll from the basket a server placed on the table and slathered it with butter. Shoving a bite into his mouth, he chewed lazily while he watched her.

"Well, actually, I did use my training in environmental engineering on an irrigation project. I certainly wasn't in charge, but I had to know what I was doing in order to be useful. But eventually I was more useful helping out at the orphanage. I was hurting, and I had something in common with those children."

"Ah, yes." He stretched his arm across the table and covered Lizzie's hand. "I heard about your parents. My condolences. It must have been very hard for you to lose both of them at the same time."

Was he being dense on purpose? She had lost him the same day.

Lizzie sat there with Wallace's cool hand on hers and thought about his sympathetic but hollow words.

"Thank you. It was hard. Very." She reached for a roll for something to do with her hands.

"Elizabeth, you look a million miles away." He bit into his roll again.

The waiter approached their table.

Wallace mouthed around a wad of bread. He didn't refer to the menus. "We'll have Caesar salad and steak Diane for two, the usual sides. Make sure the steak is rare. I want a bottle of Chateau Latour 1982. We'll have the wine now before dinner."

Wallace hadn't looked at the waiter and dismissed him by holding two menus out in his direction. The young man with dark brooding eyes took the menus in hand and turned to go.

"Excuse me? Sir?"

The waiter arched an eyebrow and looked at her. "Yes, madam?"

"I'd like to revise my half of the order, please." She looked directly at the waiter. "I'd prefer grilled swordfish with lemon and steamed vegetables for my entrée. Can you please make the Caesar salad for one and bring me a small green salad with the house dressing? And I'd like a Cosmopolitan before dinner."

"Shall I bring two wine glasses?" The waiter's hands fidgeted with the menus as he looked first at Lizzie, then Wallace.

"Yes, please." Lizzie smiled at the waiter.

"Well, Elizabeth, I should order a white wine for you." Wallace picked up the wine list.

"Don't bother." Lizzie touched the sleeve of Wallace's jacket.

She turned to the waiter. "I will have a glass of the red wine with dinner, thank you."

The waiter nodded and walked away.

"I like red wine with everything." This was the first time she'd had the strength to ever contradict Wallace. The flip her stomach did made her nervous waiting for his reaction.

Wallace looked pained. "You used to rely on me to order for you."

She wasn't a desperately lovesick girl any longer. She was a competent, intelligent, self-sufficient woman, and Wallace needed to acknowledge that.

"I did, didn't I? Huh. Well. I can navigate menus pretty well on my own now in several languages."

She leaned back in her chair as the waiter put a brimming martini glass of pale red liquid in front of her. After the ceremony of cork removal, pouring, swilling, tasting, nodding, Wallace held his wine glass up for a toast.

"You surprise me. I like that." He clinked her glass and drank, draining the glass by a third.

Lizzie sipped her drink and listened to Wallace talk with half an ear and relaxed. She remembered being chronically unsure of herself with him. She was so young, so inexperienced. But that was then.

"...They were wrong for me from the start. I was so blind in my youth. It should have been you. We were perfect together. You always put me first."

That got her full attention. "I did, didn't I? Huh." *And you never put me first.* Lizzie suffered a rush of self-loathing for her lack of self-esteem in her relationship with him. *Why was I such a doormat?*

The waiters placed the food before them with

decorum, as if the romaine lettuce and piece of fish were rare jewels. Wallace fussed that the steak was overdone and sent it back to the kitchen. *Well, he's going to have spit in his food for dinner. Hope it adds taste.*

Conversation during the meal centered on the food. She complimented it, and he criticized it.

There was no time to linger over coffee. "I want to select the best seats, and the performance starts in a half hour."

"I don't understand." Lizzie let him usher her out of the restaurant. "Aren't the seats reserved when you buy a ticket?"

"Not exactly, Elizabeth. First come, first serve for patrons who purchase box seats and I want the front row."

Moments after they were situated to Wallace's liking in the Great Hall, the concert began. Lizzie was mesmerized by the power of the music. Too soon for her, the final crescendo brought the endnote, and the audience applauded the conductor off the stage for the intermission.

The enjoyment of the night was lost to her guilt during the rest of the concert when Wallace insisted on remaining in front row seats despite the tradition to rotate seats with other box patrons after intermission. Lizzie imagined that the angry people behind her threw eye-daggers at her back. The music was glorious, but she kept thinking about the concert's end. She hoped they'd be the last to leave the box. She couldn't face the other people without feeling like she had stolen something from them.

****

Gliding down the Miracle Mile in the car afterward, Lizzie pondered the highs and lows of the evening with Wallace. Her hand loose in his, she was comfortable enough. But the slow admission that she no longer enjoyed Wallace's company nagged her.

"If my design is chosen for the Global Commerce Building, I'll need to be in Chicago often the next few months." He gave her hand a squeeze. "We will see each other again."

Lizzie didn't respond to his statement right away. She wished he had asked, rather than told her.

"I'm not sure that's a good idea. Ten years is a long time and we're different people now. I'm not the same girl who always put you first. I like being independent. I don't think that's what you are looking for."

"It's that John Clark, isn't it? I knew the minute I saw him at the reunion that he was trying to flaunt his imagined superiority." He kept his voice low, but it looked like it was an effort.

"Jack?" Pleasure flashed through her at the thought of the man. "This isn't about Jack and, as always, you're not listening. This is about me. I'm different. And, spending time with you this evening convinces me what we had together is in the past. I don't think I want to go back." She shivered at the strength it took to tell Wallace no. Every ounce of pain now came to the surface.

The car cruised in front of her building and stopped. The driver looked in the rear view mirror for some signal from Wallace.

Wallace looked stricken when she put her hand on the door handle.

"I'll get the doors," Wallace blurted. The driver nodded.

She stood outside in the clear brisk night and faced him. "May I kiss you, Elizabeth?"

No. Yes. I guess. She nodded.

He cupped his hands on her face, laced his fingers in her hair and pulled her face toward his.

She remembered the move well. Wallace's this-will-get-her-in-the-mood move. It was a nice memory and a nice kiss. But it didn't get her in the mood now.

When she pulled back out of the kiss abruptly he kept his eyes closed for a few seconds as if savoring it. *Not much to savor here.*

"Please let me come up for a little while, Elizabeth." His voice honey, humble. "Give me a chance to make up for whatever it is I've done to push you away. You make me nervous. I can't seem to do anything right lately when I am with you. Please."

"What you've done to me. You *actually* don't know?"

"Please let me prove that I've changed." The plaintive look on his face shook her. She looked into his brown eyes.

Lizzie had never taken her heart back despite his unforgivable abandonment. She remembered that one night when he was all that she wanted. Maybe she should hear him out and reopen the wounds. She had never had her say with him, either. If nothing else, she could forgive him.

"Okay, Wallace. Let's go sit in the lobby and talk."

Halfway around the revolving door, her phone vibrated in her purse. She fished the phone out, stepped clear into the lobby, Wallace close behind as she answered, "Charlie is that you? No, no, that's okay. I understand. No, you are not ruining my evening. I'm here for you. Don't cry Charlie. I'll be there in a few minutes. Hold on. I'll be right there."

"I'm sorry, Wallace. I have to go to him. He sounds awful. He's having a major meltdown."

"Weren't we in the middle of something here? Who the hell is Charlie?" He pulled at her arm to bring her closer.

"Charlie is my friend. He's very fragile right now. Remember, I told you about him and his wife, Mari's death? He needs me and I'm going." She tugged her arm away.

His brow creased and temper flared in his eyes. "All right, if you must." He inhaled a deep breath and his expression brightened. It struck her as phony. "Elizabeth, see me for breakfast tomorrow. My flight is at noon. We'd have time."

"I don't really eat breakfast, Wallace. But thanks for the invitation and for the evening."

She hurried toward the security desk without a thought to whether he followed.

He caught her by the arm stopping her. "Have coffee with me then."

"I really can't. I have plans. By the time I'm done you'll be on your plane."

I've got to get to Charlie.

"Can I call you next time I'm in the city?"

"Sure. That would be fine." *I'll finally have my say.*

She rushed to the desk and asked Byron to hail a cab.

"Don't bother," he ordered the security guard.

"Take my car Elizabeth."

"Are you sure? Can Byron hail a cab for you?"

"No. I think I could use a good brisk walk tonight."

"Thanks. Sorry to rush off like this."

"Me, too. I will call you."

****

It was well after midnight when Lizzie got home, she noticed the message light on her answer machine, "Call me whenever you get this." Kay's tone sounded odd.

Boston's an hour ahead. I can't call her this late.

Lizzie didn't want to talk to anyone now, not even her best friend. Depressed over the lackluster evening with Wallace she had no desire to rehash it.

And why had Charlie called? In complete control and downright gracious by the time she got there, he had offered her fresh brewed coffee and a slice of Eli's cheesecake. Relieved, but confused, she didn't know if she was sorry or thankful that Charlie had cried wolf and interrupted her planned confrontation with Wallace.

She burrowed into bed. Wallace was the reason sleep evaded her again.

Chapter Twelve

The tall man pushed through the revolving door and made it to Byron's security desk in two strides. He placed some flowers on the console and held out his right hand.

"Hi. We haven't met." He gazed at the nametag pinned to the left above the guard's vest pocket. "Byron, I'm Jack Clark. Nice to meet you. I'm here to see Elizabeth Moran on 43."

Bryon liked his shake, firm and honest.

"Nice to meet you, too, Mr. Clark. Go on up. I'll tell her you're on the way."

"Thanks, Byron. Call me Jack."

Byron released a lever behind the desk that allowed Jack to swing through the door to the elevator bank. The guard picked up the phone and then he noticed the flowers on the console.

He grabbed them and veered out from behind the desk to catch Jack. Poking his head through the door. "Mr. Clark? Jack? You forgot your flowers." He held the bouquet out.

"Oh, yeah." Jack walked back toward Byron. "Those are for Darla. She was on duty the last time I was here. She really liked the ones I brought for Ms. Moran, so I brought some for her."

Nice guy. Usually we're all invisible down here.

"Oh. Okay. I'll give them to her when she comes

on later. We switched shifts today."

"Thanks." Jack waited for some people to get off an elevator and walked into the car.

Byron walked back to the desk, referred to the owner list and dialed a number.

More like it if you ask me.

"Miz Moran? This is Byron at the front desk. You have a visitor…"

****

"Thank you Byron. I'll be right down." Lizzie grabbed her coat and purse, checked her face in the hall mirror one last time and opened the door. "Good girl, Marty. You stay there, I'll be back soon."

"Eager are we?" Jack smiled with his hand raised to knock.

"Oh! You scared me to death." She leaned against the doorjamb, her hand pressed to her chest. "I was on my way down to meet you."

He gazed at her, expectant.

"Did you want to come in?"

"Yep. Just for a minute." Nudging her back inside, he closed the door behind him and handed her a wrapped present.

He bent to pet Marty. "Go ahead and open it before we leave."

"What's this for?" She threw her coat over her shoulder and tore at the paper.

"You'll love it." Marty laid flat on her back, lolling in ecstasy as Jack scratched her belly.

Lizzie wadded the paper and tossed it on the counter. She held a tiny dog sweater in her hand and exclaimed, "A Bear's sweater? Get this thing out of my house!" She waved it at him.

He didn't stop his petting. "Marty likes da Bears."

Marty cocked her head at Jack.

"You see? She smiled at me."

"You're awful." Lizzie put the sweater on the counter. "You can't put it off any longer, Jack. Time to pay up. I'm starving."

The dinner rush hadn't yet started at the restaurant. A hostess greeted them. Jack pointed to a high table with bar chairs situated in the window. "Can we have that table, please?"

The hostess hesitated. "Well…actually. Somebody just called and asked me to hold that table. But…we really don't take reservations here, so if you want it, I guess I can give it to you. You were here first."

The hostess walked toward the window table.

"No. That's okay." Jack looked toward the rear of the restaurant. "How about a booth in the back?"

"Sure." She reversed and walked to the rear of the restaurant.

Minutes later, they were sitting in a booth when a beaming, buxom woman in her forties sashayed over. "You handsome devil, where have you been hiding?"

She patted Jack's shoulder, scooted Lizzie over on the wooden bench with gentle nudges of her ample hips and sat next to her, smiling at Jack on the other side of the booth. "Who's your lady?"

"Rae, you gorgeous woman," Jack declared. "Beth Moran, meet Rachael Johnson."

Rachael put her arm around Lizzie and hugged her against her warm pillowy body. "Hi, Beth."

She wasn't used to strangers calling her Beth or hugging her, either. But instantly she was comfortable with the friendly waitress. "Hi, Rachael."

"Call me Rae." She popped back up on her feet, pulled a pencil from behind her ear and took a small pad from the back pocket of her black jeans. "This one's a keeper, Jacky. Too skinny, though. Let's feed her fast."

"She's a keeper all right. Likes football, has a mean backswing and a pink-bellied dog who adores me." Jack handed over the menus. "But we're from separate worlds. She likes Green Bay."

Rae looked scandalized. "Bite your tongue! Don't you be bringing this woman here to watch any games. I'd fear for her life."

The waitress laughed. "So. What can I get you?"

"We'd like a carafe of Merlot and some cheddar cubes to start. Does that sound all right to you, Beth?"

"What are cheddar cubes?" Lizzie loved trying new food.

Jack mimicked Rae who looked at her with an open mouth. "The woman has never had cheddar cubes, Rae."

Rae patted Lizzie's hand. "Probably the girl doesn't want to have a heart attack before she's forty. Stuff goes straight to the arteries."

"I'd rather eat them than live another couple of years," Jack confessed. "You game, Beth?"

"Sure, bring 'em on." She folded her hands on top of the table.

"Okay. And we'll have a medium Malnati's salad and a large pan sausage. You like sausage pizza, Beth, or would you like something else?"

"I love sausage pizza. Especially at Lou's. But large?" She shook her head.

"A starving man orders large and takes home

leftovers. Hey, if we have room we can have a cookie pizza for dessert."

"Atta boy. Fatten the girl up. I'll be right back with your drinks."

Lizzie went to freshen up. When she came back, Rae and Jack were bantering as Rae set the drinks and the appetizer on the table. On impulse, Liz slid her slim digital camera out of a side pocket of her purse, composed the shot and took a picture. Jack smiled and Rae blinked several times in her direction.

"You taking my picture? Give me that camera and get over here, girl. I'll take a picture of you two." Rae accepted the camera from Lizzie. "Is this thing hard to work?"

"Point and shoot." Taking the camera back Lizzie identified a button on top with her index finger. "Just push this when you're ready."

Lizzie handed the camera over and stood next to where Jack sat. He put his arm around her waist. Before Rae snapped the picture, Jack pulled Lizzie onto his lap. She laughed and circled her arms around his neck, an uninhibited hug.

Rae set the camera on the table. "You'll show that picture to your kids someday." She left them alone.

Holy cow, kids. She pushed her hair behind her ear. Kids? Lizzie got off Jack's lap and sat in the booth. "Do you ever want kids, Jack?"

She picked up a cheddar cube and popped it in her mouth. "Mmmmm. This is delicious."

"Fried cheese. Nothing like it." Jack ate one, too. "I already have a passel of kids." He took another and washed it down with wine.

"You have kids? Mari never mentioned anything

about kids when she spoke of you."

"I'm supporting roughly half of the elementary school population of Guatemala. Mari was always after me to support her orphanage kids. I could never say no to her. Or to them, either, every time she showed me another picture. I even learned some Spanish so I could write letters to them."

Fascinated, she helped herself to more cheese. "That's great. Ever want kids of your own?" She wasn't about to let him change the subject.

"Never really thought about it." He didn't look her in the eye.

"I've always wanted children. At least two. I was an only child who always longed for a brother or a sister."

"I have a brother you can have," he deadpanned.

"I always wanted a little sibling rivalry, too." She laughed. "How is Charlie? He was so distraught Saturday night when he called me. I had to rush over there and cut my date with Wallace short. Charlie seemed to be better by the time I got to his house. I still worry about him. Did you see him last weekend at all?"

Jack looked baffled. "Yeah, we watched football together on Sunday. He never mentioned that he had a problem or that you were there. He seemed fine to me."

"I'm glad." Glad that it cut everything short.

"So how is old Wally? Is he the candidate to give you those minimum two kids?"

The truth hit her the instant she contemplated her answer. It made her wistful. "I suspect that Wally isn't good father material. I mean Wallace." Lizzie laughed. "You don't like Wallace, do you, Jack. Why is that?"

"I know his type." He played with this wine glass.

Rae brought the salad and Jack heaped some on a glass plate and handed it to Lizzie before he helped himself.

"Really? What type is that?" How thoughtful to serve her first.

"Can't trust him."

"You may be right." She propped her chin in her hand and watched Jack eat. "Mind if I ask a personal question?"

He looked up with an amused look. "No harm in asking." He resumed his food absorption.

"Have you ever been serious with a woman, Jack?"

"Not really. I lean toward good friends with benefits." His dark eyes were teasing. "I've never had too much faith in that kind of thing."

"What kind of thing?" She put another cheese cube in her mouth.

****

He chuckled. "Your kind of thing." *Marriage, kids, empty promises.*

"I don't get it."

"Pretty lady, let's change the subject. How's the salad?"

"Maybe I do get it. You're not into commitment. So stereotypically male." She rolled her eyes.

Male? You never met my mother. He arched an eyebrow, but didn't respond.

"You called me 'pretty lady.' You think I'm pretty?"

He smiled at her fishing for compliments. "You're enjoying this, aren't you?" He skimmed the back of her elbow with his thumb. "Yes, I think you're pretty in a scrawny way."

"You're really handsome."

The compliment pleased him inordinately stoking an inner fire. But he didn't need to fish for compliments. "You say that because I called you pretty. Now eat."

She sampled the salad. "My God, Jack, this is delicious. It has little pieces of fried salami in it. And cheese. I'm not sure it's a good thing that I've discovered these dishes."

"You could use some meat on those bones."

"I am not skinny."

Actually he'd like to get her out of that sweater and settle the debate.

She stuffed a big forkful in her mouth that bulged her cheeks. Her jaw worked drawing his eyes to her lips. Lush, inviting, nothing skinny about them.

****

Slowly sipping wine, Lizzie relished the way he looked at her. Her insides warmed from more than the wine. The man obviously didn't want forever with a woman, but there was no mistaking that he wanted her now.

Why didn't that make her furious? Wasn't Wallace just like that? Probably. And it had nearly destroyed her. Commitment issues or not, there was no harm in learning more about gorgeous Jack. "So what takes the place of relationships? Work?"

"Maybe. Sometimes. If you love what you do." He polished off the last of the salad on his plate.

"I understand. I love what I do with a passion. Do you love what you do?" The wine caused a pleasant light-headedness.

"Oh, yeah." He wiped his mouth with a napkin.

"There are so many dimensions to my work. I'm never bored. Last week I was involved in a bid for the GC Building. That is a very exciting project."

"And if you win the bid, you'll build it?"

"Yes. First the architectural design has to be approved and then blueprints drawn up. A whole lot of bureaucracy in the middle follows. Then I'll build it."

"Right. Do you happen to know if the architect for a building gets involved in its actual construction?"

"The good ones do. Why?"

"I was thinking about Wallace."

Jack's eyes darkened. "I'm sure the only way he's involved in construction is to skim off the top of construction bids."

"Jack! What a thing to say. Let's not talk about Wallace anymore. I'm sorry I brought him up."

The pizza came and she dug in. Somewhere, Lizzie found the room to stuff in a gigantic, thick-crusted slice blanketed with sausage and dripping with cheese. Jack ate a slice and picked up the pie server to dish out another for each of them, but Lizzie covered her plate with her hands.

"*No más*. I'm about to burst." She leaned her back against the wood booth, wine glass in hand, and sighed in satisfaction.

Lizzie observed him as he ate. With total focus, he neatly vacuumed in the food obviously uninhibited in his enjoyment. Open and free, she didn't care about *commitments* in the least. Pure fun. Why couldn't she have fun with a man? Full, not just with food, but also with joyous possibility. When had she ever been daring? Certainly in her work. But in her social life?

"Jack, why are you here with me tonight?"

135

He furrowed his brow. "Because the Bears suck."

"There's that. But why would you want to take me out just because of a bet? You could have shelled out money instead."

His brow furrowed tighter. He put down his knife and fork, settled back on his side of the booth and contemplated her. His keen expression and wide blue eyes convinced her that his response would be honest. "I like you. You help people you know and people you don't know. I respect that."

He reached across the table and held both her hands.

Lizzie focused on their hands linked together, a powerful, sensual connection that sped up her heart and made her squirm in her seat. She wondered if he could sense the current running through her when he touched her.

Magnetism pulsed in his dark, dark eyes. "Besides. I had to reciprocate for your football party."

Another rush now of tenderness mixed with sexual zingers. "That's sweet, Jack. Thank you. But I'm the one who's grateful. I had a wonderful time at the reunion because of you."

Bending his head, he stroked her arm lightly with his hand.

"Because Wally was jealous?" His eyes fixed on hers. The pointed question swirled in their charcoal blue depths.

"No, Jack. Because of you. It was wonderful getting to know you. I would like to get to know you better."

He half stood and leaned toward her planting a kiss on her lips that pressed her back in the booth, arms relaxed at her sides.

****

Jack regretted the impulse. Even though he had instigated the kiss, he was powerless in its hold. She kissed him back, her floral scent and lips that tasted of sweet wine, overtook him. He forgot his surroundings and explored her lips and mouth with his tongue. Beth's mouth was the only part of her body he touched, but just this small exquisite touch could plunge him over the edge.

He had to break the hold, rein in this powerful desire. Reluctantly, he sat back.

He composed his face, even though it seemed he was reconfiguring every cell in his body to do it. The innocent gleam in her eyes was still there, even more so now. She looked at him unblinking. Dark green smoke swirled in those emerald eyes.

Jack had seen it before and understood the unspoken invitation to kiss her again. He wanted to, this time all over her body, wanted to taste her and immerse in the garden scent that clung to her. Tempting.

We're both consenting adults, why not? We could go back to her place. And this time we won't watch sporting events on her flat screen TV.

He gazed into her sweet and so seductive face.

She's practically a virgin. Would I be there in the morning for her? No. That would put me in the same league as Wally. Can't do it.

"Sorry. I shouldn't have done that," he placed both his hands flat on either side of his plate. "We should give them the table."

Scarlet welts colored her cheekbones. Beth looked at him blankly and didn't speak as she gathered her things.

Jack signaled to Rae. She brought their bill and Jack left cash on top of it. Beth stood and Jack helped her with her coat before he donned his and steered her outside.

He kept her close, his arm around her to insulate her against the frigid wind. By the time they walked the four short blocks from the restaurant to Beth's building, the inside of his nose stung and his eyes watered from the cold. But his gut burned wanting more of her.

Outside the building, he wrapped her in his arms fanning the inner flames higher. He put his hand under her chin and turned her face gently upward so she could see his eyes—hoping that they projected that he cared about her feelings. Because he did, he wouldn't risk hurting her with a casual affair. In the soft glow of the lobby lights reflected on the pavement, he kissed her softly on the forehead. "Goodnight, Beth."

"Thank you for dinner. Goodnight, Jack."

****

The cold did nothing to dampen the fire from his kiss at the restaurant. Lizzie longed to taste the thrill of his lips against hers again instead of a soft peck on the forehead. But this wasn't the place. Now wasn't the time.

Inside she raised one hand in a wave, and he waved back, then strode away, sexy as hell, his hands in the pockets of his leather jacket.

Turning around Lizzie noticed Darla grinning at her from her security post.

"Hi Darla."

"Hi, Miz Moran. Your man brought me these flowers." She pointed to a bowl of tulips on the counter.

"My man? He did?" Lizzie stepped closer to smell the flowers. "Wasn't that nice?"

"Yes, ma'am. Nobody ever brought me flowers here before. You be sure to thank him for me, will you?"

"I will, Darla, first chance I get." *If he calls and I get the chance at all. I really hope he calls.*

****

Lizzie kicked off her shoes and dropped her purse on the floor in the living room. Ambient city lights glowed around her, a source of joy and awe to her every night, like living with an enormous Christmas tree in your living room all year long.

She walked to the window and appreciated the view of her "back yard" for a while, her thoughts muddled. Last week she had looked out at the same lights and thought about Wallace. After the evening with Jack, Wallace had somehow gotten replaced in her reverie.

If she had invited Jack home with her, would she be lying across her bed that minute? Lizzie closed her eyes and pictured what it might be like, his powerful hands on her breasts, and his breath on her neck. She crossed her arms in front of her chest and grasped her upper arms suddenly cold, alone.

She'd call Kay. They had played phone tag all week, and Lizzie needed to hear Kay's voice.

Mick picked up.

"Hey, Mick. How's the daddy-to-be doing?"

"I'm fine, Lizzie girl, but I miss my Katherine."

"What? Where's Kay?"

"Shit. She wanted to tell you herself. I thought you knew. She's in the hospital. She started spotting, and the doctor ordered full bed rest. He wants to delay delivery as long as possible. The babies benefit from every additional day. She tried to stay in bed here but couldn't do it. I'm working all the time on the renovations to get everything done by the time the babies are born. She can't handle my working and waiting on her, too. The hospital is the only place where she can be controlled." He laughed. "It's good she's there, but I miss her, especially at night."

Oh God. I don't like the sound of this. "Should I come out there, Mick? Does she need me?"

"Oh, no. She's fine. But I'll bet she'd love to talk to you. Try her now. I'm sure she's still up."

He gave her the number of the hospital. "Thanks, Mick. I'll call her right after we hang up. Good night."

Kay was awake and answered the phone on the first ring. "Hi again, Michael. I miss you so much, too."

"I miss you back, and so does Mick."

"Lizzie! Hi, Bella. I guess Mick told you the deal with me. Doesn't it just suck? Thank God I like to read. I'm gobbling down books by the dozen. Hospital food is completely inedible, though. Fortunately there's no room in this body for food."

Relieved that she sounded normal, Lizzie counseled, "You just do what they tell you to do so you have big, fat babies to love in a couple of months."

"I know, I know. So. What's going on with you? How was the fa-fa symphony with Wallace?"

Lizzie relaxed, reassured by Kay's enthusiasm for girl talk. "The symphony with Wallace was fa-fa. It was all right. Nice, I guess. He can be so bossy and self-centered sometimes. I told him I didn't want to see him anymore. But then he apologized, claims he's changed.

I decided to hear him out, maybe have my say, but Charlie's call interrupted that. Charlie needed me and that came first."

"Honey, I think I'm glad for the interruption. Are you sure you want to get that involved with Wallace again?"

"I'm not sure of anything when it comes to men. But then when Jack kissed me tonight, I wanted him to keep kissing me."

A garbled female voice in the background. Kay's words muted, unintelligible.

Alarm pierced her. "Kay are you all right? What's going on?"

"It's nothing," her voice clear in Lizzie's ear. "Just the nurse taking my blood pressure."

Lizzie exhaled with whoosh.

"No, I don't need a thing. Yes, thank you," came Kay's muted voice. Then loud and clear, "What's today? Saturday? That's right, you had a date with Jack tonight."

"Not technically a date. He was paying off a bet. I just got home. I had a wonderful time. He brought Marty a Bears sweater just to tease me, and we ate cheddar cubes, salad and sausage pizza. And he brought flowers for the security guard."

"It sounds like you had a better time with Jack. Where does this leave Wallace?"

"I don't know. They're very different. Jack is an amazing kisser." *And he doesn't demand tables, order me around or talk to me like I'm five.*

"Sounds pretty unconfused to me. I remember that lip-lock at the reunion. Amazing seems like the right adjective. Are you going to see Jack again?"

"I'm not sure. He didn't say one way or the other. Kay, I sure hope so."

Lizzie stared at the city lights and thought about a man who learned Spanish to write to little kids and brought flowers to ladies he hardly knew.

"I miss you, Kay. I wish we lived closer."

"I miss you, too, sweetie. I can't wait until January when these babies are born. Then we can be together for a nice, long visit."

Chapter Thirteen

Lizzie pushed the "down" elevator button. The conversation with Kay disturbed her. She had wrestled with the bedcovers all night thinking about her best friend and trying to shake her sense of foreboding. Mick sounded more worried than he let on. Come to think of it, Kay never once mentioned her need for chocolate.

Something was wrong. She would just have to keep in closer contact with her for the next two months.

Distracted, she waved to Henry, who was always on duty Sunday mornings, and headed out. A Great Lakes cold wind slammed into her. Slipping her fingers into her gloves, she bent to adjust the tie on her sneaker. A taxi turned off Kinsey Street and pulled up next to her.

Wallace, dressed head to toe in package-creased, running gear, jumped out and paid the driver. "Good morning," he hailed her. "I hoped you were still a creature of habit."

She eyed his jogging outfit. "Yep, I jog. New clothes?"

"Well, Elizabeth, not exactly the welcome I had hoped. I remembered your need to run every day at the crack of dawn. Since you were called away and our time together was cut short the last time I was in town, I thought you might let me tag along. Remember the

143

mornings along the Charles?"

"I remember how you hated to get up and meet me in the mornings. How you would spend the first half hour grumbling. How you said, 'Never on Sundays.' You do know it's Sunday. Right, Wallace?"

"See the sacrifice I am making to spend time with you, Elizabeth? Let me join you, and I promise not to grumble."

He smiled that smile that used to melt her heart. Probably more handsome now than he had been in college, she truly had loved him. Faced with him now, she couldn't imagine why.

Although he seemed very interested in her. Why wasn't that satisfying? Could she sum it up in four letters: J-A-C-K?

Jack changed everything, showed her how a woman should be treated. Her blood sizzled every time he was near, something that Wallace didn't do, in fact, had never done. But, she reminded herself, Jack didn't make commitments, either.

"Earth to Elizabeth. Are we going to run, or are we going to be found hours from now frozen to the pavement?"

Lizzie shook her head, focused on Wallace's face. "Yes, sorry. Let's go."

"I'm a tourist. Lead the way." He waved his arm in front of him.

She jogged off, set the pace and before long she kept a smooth cadence with him at her side.

Lizzie loved this time of day. Most people were snuggled under their down comforters. On mornings like this, Chicago was all hers. Except today. Resigned to sharing her time with Wallace, she hoped the endorphin rush would erase her irritation with him for horning in uninvited on her quiet time. In the Sunday morning calm, traffic lights changed colors without effect, no cars to obey them. Uninterrupted, she jogged steadily toward the looming gates of Navy Pier.

"Is something wrong?"

Lizzie had almost forgotten Wallace was there. "I'm worried about Kay."

"What's wrong with Kay?" His words came in staccato bursts as he jogged.

Not winded at all Lizzie replied, "She's in the hospital on total bed rest. I spoke with her last night. She made it sound routine, and that's logical since she's carrying twins. Still. I really don't know."

"She looked as healthy as a horse, and I mean a horse, at the reunion. Women have babies every day, Elizabeth. Don't worry about her."

His tone and the deprecating remark about Kay's size convinced her it was worthless to discuss Kay or her feelings with Wallace. He only cared about himself.

Sneakers slapped a steady rhythm against the pavement lulling her into a familiar silence. She remembered when Wallace's company used to exhilarate her.

Back when he had been trying to get her into his bed, he had been very attentive. He'd show up at her dorm and wait sleepy-eyed against a tree until she came out. Their runs had usually lasted about an hour. Once he had finished with his preliminary grumbling, they'd hit their stride and jog along in comfortable silence.

Afterward over spinach and Swiss cheese omelets, he'd hold her hand and listen to her conversation as if he cared about what she thought, felt. Had he? Had she mattered to him or were her memories stilted?

"You know what I would like right now? A plate-size spinach omelet oozing with Swiss cheese."

Lizzie stopped jogging and faced him when he halted a couple strides ahead of her. "I was just this minute thinking of the Greenhouse."

"We had some good times, didn't we, Elizabeth?" He closed the gap between them, only inches away.

She smelled soap, the mild tang of perspiration. "We did."

"If only we could go back in time. Maybe things would be different." He looked down at the pavement. "I would never hurt you again." Wallace raised his head and gazed at her face. A shaky smile stretched the corners of his lips.

She looked into his eyes and couldn't help returning the smile, unable to forget that she had loved him once with all her heart. Despite the devastation he had caused her, she had never hated him. It had taken her most of the past ten years to rebuild what he had destroyed in her, though. She wouldn't fall for his innocent act again.

"Let's just run, Wallace."

"No pressure, Elizabeth, no pressure." He released her hand.

Lizzie checked her watch. "Time to head back." Pivoting, she reversed and Wallace fell in stride.

"Want to grab some breakfast?"

Lizzie glanced toward him, met his eyes. "I'm sorry, I can't."

"Have a date?"

"The same date I have every Sunday morning. Church." She turned forward, her attention on the curving trail skirting the lakeshore rimmed with skyscrapers, an awesome sight.

"Oh, you still do that?"

"Wallace, I've told you a million times it's not something I do, it's who I am. How come you never understand that?"

"Maybe I just never bothered to try."

Wallace had never owned up to a gap in understanding before.

"I'm surprised you can be that honest."

"I'm insulted, Elizabeth. I've changed. Honesty is extremely important to me now."

"That's good." *Not sure if you're capable of being sincere about anything.*

Stopping at the circular drive that fronted her building he asked, "How about a rain check for breakfast the next time I'm in town?"

Her thoughts the past week had veered toward not seeing him again.

"I'll be honest. I doubt that you've changed, although you say differently. I told you at dinner that I don't think I'm what you're looking for. Truthfully, I don't think you're what I'm looking for, either."

"What is there to think about? You loved me. I made a mistake, and I'm determined to make up for it."

He grasped the sides of her arms and in a split second his lips touched hers. Shocked, she didn't yank away immediately, testing the possibility that the kiss would spark a fiery sizzle and trigger some chemistry of attraction. It didn't.

Turning her face sideways, she broke the kiss. "It was nice running with you, but I have to go."

"I'll call you." A slight whine rang in his tone.

"That's fine. Safe trip home."

Approaching her building, she didn't look back as she entered.

****

Lizzie fluffed her hair and left her bedroom at full speed. Marty had been in a playful mood that made Lizzie have to rush to get ready for morning services after she threw toys for the dog to chase.

Tired from playing, she tossed a cookie to the snoozing pup for later and hurried out.

She had discovered Assumption Church her first week after moving to Chicago. A little jewel, it wasn't fancy on the outside, but the interior was magnificent with its glorious stained glass, rosy marble, gilded flourishes and incandescent frescoes. No matter what troubles she hauled to church, she left them at the door finding only peace within those walls.

Selecting her usual seat in the first pew she sat back and gazed at the enormous stained glass depiction of the assumption of Mary over the altar. It was warm here despite the inadequacy of the heating system. Bathed in the spill of light from rows of ornate chandeliers above her, she was still.

Candles lit, the organist played a prelude, and she waited for the special serenity of the place to wash over her. It didn't come.

Please keep Kay safe. I couldn't bear it if I lost her. Why did I pray so long for Wallace to come back to me? I think I've been wasting your time.

Lizzie's inner disquiet continued.

Jack. I can't get him out of my mind.

When Mass ended, she left the church comforted and refreshed. A light touch on her elbow turned her into Jack's warmth.

"Beth, I thought it was you." His smile lit his eyes.

"Jack." She took his appearance as a heavenly sign. "What a wonderful surprise."

He wore casual clothes and a denim jacket; his black hair messy and his cheeks flushed dull pink from the wind.

"I drove over to my gym, but it was closed today because of some water crisis. I went looking for coffee and saw that I had time to catch Mass here. I've never been in this church before. Beautiful interior design elements."

"I found it when I first got to Chicago, and I've come here ever since."

"It seems like you know this town better than someone who was born and raised here. Namely me."

"I've had a lot of time alone to wander the streets and see different things. I found something new a while ago. If you have a few hours free later, I can show it to you."

****

Something about her made him want to drop everything. Unaccustomed to acting on impulse, Jack still jumped at her invitation, "I'm intrigued. What time does the adventure begin?"

"Pick me up at five. Dress warm. We'll be walking."

"Okay then. Do you want a ride home?"

"No, thanks. I like to walk. See you later."

Moving rapidly down the block away from him, Beth looked like a teenager in black jeans and a fur trimmed bomber jacket, so unlike any of the much more lush, full-bodied women who usually attracted him. He had a splendid view of her retreating figure. He stood and appreciated it for a while before he walked around the building to the church parking lot.

That kiss over the pizza pan proved his attraction to her didn't fall into any of his usual categories. Even women like Gina didn't make him crazy with lust after one kiss, or ten. He was losing it over Beth Moran.

A couple of kisses and passes around a dance floor? How the hell did that translate into a fire in his gut and an invasion of his thoughts?

Jack had been thinking about her when he happened on the little church. He hadn't noticed her until Communion was served, and he'd seen her walk forward to the altar. His inner leap of excitement at the coincidence that she was there both delighted and scared him.

His head told him it might be time for a friendly parting before his emotions got the best of him. But he hadn't hesitated to accept her invitation for that evening. He had told her the truth and was intrigued. No doubt Beth was a heart stealer, like Mari, like his mother. If he was upfront with her and she agreed to no strings, they could part as friends eventually.

****

The sunset was painted in pastel layers of purple, pink and gray across the sky to their left as Lizzie set out on foot with Jack that evening. Dim stars poked out in the darkening sky and the frosty November air chilled the lungs.

She laced her arm through his, snuggled into him for warmth and walked north on Dearborn. "I really had a great time last night. I enjoyed meeting Rae and the food was just delicious. I have new favorites to order.

Thank you."

"Don't thank me. Thank your Packers. Double or nothing next game?"

"You're on."

"Have you talked to Kay or Mick lately?" Jack's gloved hand covered hers linked around his bicep.

"Kay's in the hospital."

"What happened?" His brows pinched with concern.

"Nothing, really, according to Mick. The doctor wanted her to have complete bed rest. The house is chaos because the renovations aren't finished, and the hospital is the best place for her."

"But?"

"But I have this nagging feeling that something is wrong, and I can't seem to talk or pray myself out of it."

"Is there anything I can do to help? Kay and Mick are really good people."

His concern for her friends and consideration of her feelings touched her. Especially after Wallace treated her apprehensions as nonsense. Jack had only spent a few days with Kay and Mick. Wallace and Kay had grown up together. Yet Jack offered to help and didn't make her feel foolish for worrying.

Comforted that she wasn't alone against this wall of dread she said, "Thanks so much for offering. I hope I'm worrying for nothing."

They were nearing Charlie's neighborhood in Lincoln Park.

"Are we going to see my brother?"

"Nope." Lizzie shook her head.

"Well, the only place I know over here besides

Charlie's is the zoo. Are we going to the zoo?"

"Yep."

"Is it even open at night?"

"You'll see."

Quickening the pace, she led him to the zoo. Lizzie grabbed Jack's hand and tugged him through the wide-open, main gate, "Ta da." She spread her arms, mittens dangling. "Welcome to *Zoolights*."

Open-mouthed, Jack took in the light-encrusted trees that blazed around them like magical torches, a child's fantasyland.

"How could I have missed this from the street?" He glanced back toward the gate at the dark foliage that rimmed the park and kept *Zoolights* secreted away.

Lizzie enjoyed his reaction. He wore a wonderful star struck expression and she had a glimpse of what Jack might have been as a boy.

"Isn't this just the *coolest* thing?"

"Makes me feel like I'm four years old. How did you find this?"

"Last year one of the news stations did a story about it. I'm a sucker for anything to do with Christmas, so as soon as the show went off, I bundled myself up and headed here. I'm addicted. I must have come back twenty times last year. I even brought Mari here once. It was so special."

Her voice caught in her throat and she looked at Jack, helpless to stem tears from welling. His eyes told her he understood.

"Anyway." She dabbed her eyes with her mittens. "I couldn't wait for it to open again this year. Come on."

He didn't resist as she pulled him along by the

hand like a mommy with her happy toddler.

"There's more," she promised.

Lizzie found a bench that overlooked a huge display of *The Twelve Days of Christmas*. She sat and tugged him down next to her

Red and green lights reflected on his face as he brushed a light kiss on her cheek. "Thank you for bringing me here," he said, his voice husky.

"You're welcome." Lizzie scooted over on the bench drawn by his radiant body heat, shoulder to shoulder.

"Doesn't this kick-start your holiday spirit?" She leaned her head against his shoulder and gazed at the lights, peaceful and dreamy.

"It does. I can't believe that this has been here and I never knew about it."

"It's one of my favorite Christmas traditions now. I plan to be here every year."

"Sounds like a good plan." Jack toyed with the buttons on her coat.

Her chin toward her chest, she longed for him to undo those buttons and slip that huge, warm hand inside her coat and find her breast.

She shivered from the reaction his simple touch invoked.

"You're freezing. Let's get moving," he surmised, totally off the mark. He stood and then hoisted her to her feet.

With Jack's arm around her on the walk beneath glittering trees, she leaned close to his chest, wistfully leaving the Christmas wonderland behind.

"Do you want me to flag down a cab?"

Lizzie didn't want the closeness to end as quickly

as a cab ride back. She shook her head. "No, let's walk."

Choosing another way home, she approached the Music Hall of the Performing Arts. Jack slipped his arm from around her shoulder and pointed out a banner across the building's façade that advertised an upcoming charity ball.

Lizzie stopped and read it out loud, "The tenth annual ball sponsored by Butterfly Books and JP Hamilton Associates. Benefiting the Mariposa Leukemia Foundation."

A list of various other company sponsors included banks, legal firms, construction companies, furniture movers and real estate firms.

"This is wonderful. I didn't know Charlie was doing this. Did you know about this?"

"Of course. I just assumed you knew all about it. My company is sponsoring, too."

Lizzie nodded, scanning the list of construction companies.

"Want to go?" Jack's tone casual, off-handed.

"Yes. I'll call Charlie in the morning to get my ticket."

"Sorry, it's sold out," he said.

She faced Jack and shrugged, "Oh. I guess all I can do is make a donation."

Shoving his hands in his pockets, he cast her a playful grin, "I have two tickets. Want to go to the ball with me?"

Happy anticipation filled her. "I would love to. Thank you."

Accepting his outstretched hand, the walk resumed as the temperature outside continued to dip. Despite the frigid air, Lizzie's temperature spiked with Jack near. Twin wispy clouds of breath emitted from their mouths in front of them as if they were wading through steam on the return to her condo.

"I liked your surprise. Thanks." He brought first one of her mittens, then the other to his lips.

His warm breath fanned her numb fingertips beneath the wool and made them sting.

She tilted her head up to him. "You're welcome. I had a wonderful time sharing it with you."

"I'll call you with details about the charity ball."

Lost in his sapphire eyes, spellbound, Lizzie whispered, "I'll be waiting."

She started to move away from him, and he pulled her back into a comforting embrace. His chilled lips pressed and opened hers to the delicious heat of his mouth. The now familiar jolt of pleasure seared her senses. He made her oblivious to anything but the fresh mint taste of his lips, his musky smell, and his sensual power over her. Strange and tantalizing, Lizzie instinctively knew that if she surrendered she would have sexual power over him.

What then?

Chapter Fourteen

When Charlie called, Jack already had the portable phone in his hand, about to dial Beth's number. He knew she wasn't home. She had left on the first flight for New York that morning for a meeting with her editor.

He pictured the way she'd looked fidgeting next to him on the flight to Boston two months ago, paperback on her lap, spitting mad and flushed from yelling at him.

Jack could almost smell the soft floral perfume she always wore. The memory of it tightened the pit of his stomach. Crazy. He told himself a dozen times a day that she wasn't for him. She wanted marriage, kids. He wasn't looking for forever, didn't believe it existed. How could Beth believe in it? Prescott wasn't proof enough for her that forever is a fairy tale?

Prescott. Is that what the attraction to Beth is about? Beating Prescott at his own game?

No. Business was one thing.

Despite Jack's fierce dedication to gain a competitive edge over all business opponents, he didn't play the professional game like Wally, and he'd never play games socially. Especially with Beth.

The aftereffects of their last kiss came to mind at unexpected times. Nothing about any other woman he'd known lingered the way that innocent, potent kiss did.

She shook him, unraveled the protective web of rationalizations against love he'd spun around his heart since he was a teenager. But Charlie had grown up in the same motherless house as Jack and had figured out how to give his heart freely, living the fairy tale before Mari's death.

Jack had never asked his brother if it was worth it, but he suspected he'd answer yes. Jack had thought it smart not to confuse hormones with emotional entanglements. And Jack had been very smart until now. Beth's appeal nearly stopped his heart, jammed his brain.

So he planned to call her, just to hear her voice on her voicemail recording. Then the phone rang in his hand and made him jump.

He connected on the half ring, thinking maybe it was Beth and there was some happy ESP thing going on between them.

"Hi, I was just thinking about you."

"I'm touched, Jack." Charlie's voice was hardly the soundtrack in Jack's daydream. "And I was thinking about you, too, which is why I dialed the phone."

Use the brain, Jack. Since when do I moon over women?

"Hey, Charlie. What's up?"

"A lot, actually. Can you swing by my office sometime today? I have proofs for the book that I want to show you, and I had a call from the event planner we hired. She's faxed over some menus for us to go over."

"Menus? That's way out of my league, bro."

"Me, too. Maybe we can stumble our way through it together."

Jack walked to his desk, punched a couple of keys

on his computer and brought up his calendar for the day.

"Let's see. I have a meeting with the selection committee for the GC Building over lunch. I figure that's a good sign if they're willing to feed me. I'm not sure how long that will run. How about between two and three?"

"Works for me. See ya later, and good luck at lunch."

Jack disconnected. The urge to listen to Beth's recording had passed, sane once more. He didn't have time to be so foolish. Instead, he'd go to his office and get some work done before his lunch meeting.

Putting the phone back in its charger, he grabbed his briefcase.

He walked into the JPH Building like he owned the place. In fact, he did since the death of his grandfather, Nicholas Hamilton, several years ago. His firm's office suites took up the top two floors of the building, and other business tenants occupied the sixty floors below JP Hamilton Associates.

His grandfather had designed the building when Jack was a first year architecture student, then an intern with the firm. Jack had worked on the sketches with him and was proud that many of his ideas had been incorporated into the design.

Pop had always kept a watchful eye on his daughter's boys after she abandoned them. Too many of the people Jack loved had departed. Another reason he was not looking for forever. Nothing lasted except his buildings. There wasn't a day he walked through these doors that he didn't think of the old man and miss him.

"Good morning, Mr. Clark. You look very sharp this morning."

The woman who greeted Jack insisted, as always, on referring to him as Mr. Clark. She wore formal business attire—something she also insisted on, even though the firm's dress code had become business casual long before it was trendy.

With mouse brown hair, immovable in a pageboy cut and a middle-aged body given to plumpness, she wasn't what many people would consider beautiful, but Jack did. The smile that animated her face and emanated warmth toward anyone who stood before her desk made her pretty. She lit the lounge with welcome. Jack always considered her one of the firm's biggest assets.

"Hey, Eileen. You look lovely, as usual. Big meeting at lunch. Wish me luck."

"Always, sir. Is the meeting here? Should I prepare the conference room?"

"Nope, at The Metropolitan Club over lunch. They're either giving me great news or letting me down with a whole lot of class."

"Well, good luck again. But I am sure you will not need it sir. I have complete confidence in your design."

The phone console, the sole item on her desk, bleeped, and she turned efficiently back to her work.

Jack continued down the hall to his office, greeting other members of the firm as he made slow progress.

He settled into his well-worn leather, swivel chair with roller wheels. Even while seated, he didn't like to stay in one spot for long. Rows of bookshelves atop credenzas lined the entire wall behind him and half walls on either side of him. His desk was molded acrylic, a simple rectangle with narrow legs that allowed him latitude to move underneath it and handle plans and blueprints on its large work surface. He only kept a couple of chairs in front of his desk, as he would rather confer with his staff in the conference room. This private space, which he kept pristine and uncluttered, freed him to create without distraction.

A black telephone, the only item on Jack's desk except for a small, framed photograph of him and Charlie, distracted him now. Picking up the handset, his fingers hovered over the numbers still wanting to hear Beth's voice.

Wrestling with the impulse, he didn't want to give her the wrong idea and wasn't sure what this compulsion was about. Better to leave her alone until he could get a handle on these odd feelings.

Work. Get focused.

Jack rolled his chair to a side credenza, grabbed a banded roll of paper and scooted back to mid-desk. He worked on fine-tuning the specs for the GC Building until it was time to head over to the Sears Tower for his lunch appointment.

Security in the Sears building lobby had been tight ever since 9/11. Glad he'd left enough time to go through the mandatory process of showing his driver's license at the main security desk, badge issuance, pocket emptying and metal detector screening, he accessed the elevator bank that would whiz him to the private club on the upper floors of the building.

Hushed power lunches and dizzying views in the restaurant epitomized The Metropolitan Club. Although on time, everyone else had apparently arrived since only one open seat remained at the large table of businessmen. Judging from the apparent joviality of the group, they were a drink or two ahead of him. He walked around the table, shook hands and bantered with each of the men, before he took the vacant seat.

"You'll be needing a drink, Jack." One of the men called a waiter over.

When Jack had a Guinness delivered to him, he followed the lead of all the men at the table and raised his glass.

"You've got the Global Commerce Building, Jack. Congratulations."

He savored the best beer he ever drank having beat Wally to win the business .

****

Elated as he pushed through the doors of Butterfly Books to meet with Charlie, Pop was on Jack's mind. He wore his grandfather's cuff links, symbolically taking Pop with him to the meeting, and somehow, he believed helping maneuver its positive outcome. Normally, he didn't put stock into superstition, but this time he needed any help he could get.

Here in Charlie's offices, Pop lived on, too. Their grandfather had bankrolled the publishing company for Charlie. Pop was one hell of a man, even if he had sired their mother. Jack, a familiar visitor, didn't need the receptionist to clear him into the inner offices. Charlie wasn't at his desk, so Jack wandered around the suite searching for him snagging a cup of coffee as he passed through the break room.

He found Charlie in one of the many conference rooms leaning over the long, maple table, book proofs lined around its perimeter.

Jack joined Charlie in inspecting the proofs.

"Wow. These are great. I'm blown away. Beth does phenomenal work, Charlie. Really outstanding."

"Beth?"

Jack rolled a chair back and sat. "Just a nickname that seemed to fit when I first met her. It stuck. She looks like a Beth to me."

"What exactly does a Beth look like?" Charlie sat next to him.

"You know wholesome, innocent, nothing like a Gina." He laughed when Charlie rolled his eyes.

"We both know what a Gina looks like. All body. You sure can pick them Jack."

"You can say that again. Did you know she's a Packer fan?"

"Gina?" Charlie's brow creased.

"No Beth." And she sure knows how to wear a Packer's T-shirt."

"Oh, yeah. She's a Green Bay fanatic. Mari and I brought her back a cheese-head hat when we went to a game at Lambeau Field. She loved it. Drove us crazy wearing it every time we all watched football together."

"Good God. I'm surprised she didn't wear it when we watched the Bears/Packers game together."

Charlie's eyes widened. "You watched the Bears/Packers game together?"

"Yeah, at her place, complete with a comfort food buffet. She sure can cook." Jack picked up the night shot of the JPH Building. "Wow. Look at this. How the hell did she get this shot? She must have been hanging from a helicopter."

"Actually she was. She was coming back from the train wreck in Kentucky." Charlie took the photo out of Jack's hand. "Let's get back to football at Lizzie's house. When was this?"

"A few weeks ago." Jack shook his head thinking about Beth hanging out of a plane over a conflagration. "She was flying over that chemical fire in a helicopter? More than a dozen train cars ignited. She's got a lot of courage."

****

Charlie thought about the years he'd known Lizzie. She had been fearless in Guatemala. Lizzie and Mari went into areas where there was guerilla warfare to rescue children. Lizzie was in Sarajevo and the Middle East during the Gulf War while bullets flew, traveled in tanks in Iraq. She faced a world without parents as a young adult and stood up to him when he tried to withdraw from a world without Mari.

"She has more courage than you and me put together. She's gone through a lot. It's amazing she's not bitter. Lizzie is the original softie. Even with all the assignments, she still manages to dedicate her free time to Mari's orphanage. Her pictures have raised more money than any other fundraising."

Jack looked at the photo of the JPH Building again, gestured at others on the table. "She takes the most astounding pictures. I think she was drawn to the 'necklaces' on the top of the buildings. She loves sparkly lights. Have you ever been to *Zoolights* at Lincoln Park Zoo? Beth took me to see them Sunday night. Blew me away."

I'll be damned. "You've been seeing Lizzie?"

"Let's look at the rest of these proofs."

"Not so fast. Are you and Lizzie dating each other?"

"No." Jack put the proof down and focused on the

next image. "I lost a bet and took her to Lou's for pizza. Then we met the next day at church, by chance. Whatever. When does the book come out?"

"I want to run this by Lizzie, too, but I was thinking of a book launch party on New Year's Eve." Charlie wasn't about to let this go. "What's going on with you and Lizzie?"

"Nothing. She isn't interested in me, either, so it's mutual. She still has the hots for Prescott," Jack sneered. "I do not see what she sees in that jackass. I played my part well enough to make Wally jealous."

Charlie studied Jack, read his body language detecting the "tells" that he was skirting the whole truth.

Doesn't look me in the eye, a slight raise of his shoulders. Oh he's interested all right.

"Hey, I forgot to tell you. I beat Prescott out again. I got the GC Building contract."

Charlie's head spun with Jack's quicksilver change of subject, but he returned Jack's high five. "Congratulations. You deserve it."

For now, he'd let the subject of Jack and Lizzie go. Maybe. "I'm thinking about inviting Lizzie to dinner on Thanksgiving at Grandma Viv's. She showed me I have a lot to be thankful for this year, and Grandma mentioned she would be welcome. Do you have a problem with her being at dinner?"

Jack tugged at his shirt collar. "No. Doesn't affect me either way. Do what you want."

"Think I will." Color crept up Jack's neck.

"So, anyway," Charlie continued, on thin ice with his brother. "I have an idea for the launch party. What do you say to our holding it at JPH? The book is all about your buildings. It would be the perfect venue."

"Sure. Fine. Want anybody in my shop involved with the arrangements?"

"Maybe with setting up the room. We'll take care of the guest list, invitations and arrangements for the party here at my office. All you have to do is show up."

"If you need any extra help just give Eileen a call. She'll organize it for you."

Jack stood and moved along the edge of the table until he reached the end of the row of proofs.

"So. Lizzie approved the proofs. Do I have your approval?" Charlie put a form in front of Jack for his signature.

"Of course, they're great." Jack scribbled his name on the paper under Lizzie's signature and shuffled his feet.

Charlie recognized that body language, too. "Don't bolt on me yet. We have to go over the food options for the ball. I was looking it over before you arrived. Why does everything have a special sauce and mushrooms? Let's go to my office and look at the menu."

"Okay." Jack took the lead out of the conference room. "Steak and potatoes sound good to me."

Chapter Fifteen

The buttery, cinnamon-spice smell of two freshly baked pumpkin breads cooling on a wire rack, enticed Lizzie. She stood at her stove, comfortable in an oversized pair of flannel pajamas, and stirred a spoon in a pot of chocolate milk to enjoy while watching the Macy's Thanksgiving Day parade on TV.

This was the first year in a long time she had been home for Thanksgiving. She had run away from the holiday every year since her parents died, starting with her years in Guatemala where she could ignore the non-existent holiday there with ease.

For the past few years, Kay had invited her to their family celebration, an invitation that she had always declined due to assignment conflicts. Sometimes she had legitimate work conflicts, and sometimes she had manipulated the truth a bit.

An assignment began tomorrow with a reporter from NewsWorld Magazine to return to Niger. Lizzie had hoped to leave yesterday, but the reporter wanted to be home with his children. Couldn't blame him, but it left her home alone with her memories.

Kay's mom had called her the week before to extend this year's invitation. Again, she fibbed her way out of accepting it, and claimed she would be on a plane headed for Africa. She'd kept the specifics about her departure date vague.

As much as she loved Kay, she had never wanted a substitute family on this day of the year. She might consider next year when the twins celebrate their first Thanksgiving.

Charlie's call yesterday had her racking up more fibs. He'd asked her to join him, Jack, their father and grandmother at his Thanksgiving table deciding to be a host instead of letting his grandmother cook for the family. Thrilled that Charlie felt strong enough to carry on Mari's holiday tradition, she had almost accepted, especially when he had remarked, "It might be fun for you because Jack will be here."

Odd that Charlie let that last sentence hang. *Jack.* That slow smile, his scorching kisses snuck up on her in daydreams and during her vulnerable nights. But as sisterly as she was with Charlie, there was no way she wanted to be Jack's little sister at the holiday table. Jack, after all, hadn't extended the invitation.

On this day of gratitude, she was thankful she'd met Jack. He made her reconsider her opinions of men, in general. He made her forget Wallace almost entirely. But why did he shy away from commitment? What deep dark secrets did he keep locked inside?

She could handle celebrating Thanksgiving alone, instead of pretending it away. Her mother's treasured recipe for the bread that spiced the air and made her stomach grumble had been dusted off and put to use. A turkey potpie would suffice for the main meal. She'd brave watching the parade, a first since she'd lost her parents. They'd taken her to watch the floats and the gigantic balloons several times as a child. Those happy memories tore her apart.

She had spent the last months telling Charlie to get

on with his life and instead of avoiding his traditions with Mari he should treasure them to keep her memory alive. So she'd practice what she preached to Charlie, watch the parade and enjoy one of her mother's Thanksgiving recipes.

Hot chocolate poured and a slice of bread on a plate, she settled in front of the TV. Marty secured the spot next to the coffee table, vigilant for any runaway crumbs.

The phone rang several times before she registered the need to get up and answer it.

"Happy Thanksgiving to you, too, Darla. Who? He is?" She looked down at her flannels in dismay. "Would you mind sending him up? Great. Thanks."

Damn it. Wallace was here?

Lizzie opened the door as soon as she heard the elevator bell. He walked toward her dragging his feet slightly as if hesitant. He stopped a few feet in front of her open door.

Lizzie stood in the center of the doorframe, blocking it. "Wallace you really should have called first."

"I was walking around the city. Took a chance that you'd be here. I didn't want to be alone." His hands in his coat pockets, he had a dejected expression on his face.

Wallace sounded like he wanted her to do *him* a favor by spending time with him, a surprising twist.

"What are you doing alone in Chicago? Doesn't your family have dinner plans?"

"Oh, Mother will be pained because, after all, what will people say? But really, it will just be one, empty chair at the table at the club. I will hardly be missed.

Mind if I come in, Elizabeth? Please." His head tilted, his eyes beseeched her.

"All right." She stepped aside, let him pass and closed the door. "I was just watching the parade. Give me a minute and I'll change my clothes."

"Sure smells good in here." He shrugged out of his coat and laid it over the back of a chair. "Let's watch the end of the parade together. I'll take a slice of that bread and give me some of that hot chocolate, too." His head nodded toward the pot of chocolate milk on the stove, and he leaned back against the counter in the galley kitchen, making himself at home.

Lizzie prickled at the wait-on-me implication, was about to pour the chocolate in an automatic hostess response when she dropped her hand from the pot handle and whirled on him, "I am not in the mood for this, Wallace. I didn't invite you here, and you didn't ask me if you could come. I think you should leave."

His face pained, "Don't throw me out, please. I had a depressing week."

Exasperated, she'd hear him out since she didn't know what else to do with him. "I'll bite. What happened?"

"I lost the bid for the building here. I found out yesterday."

"That's too bad. Surely there'll be other projects."

"I put all my efforts for the last few months into it, and then I'm beaten again by JP Hamilton. The GC building would really have made a difference to my company. Father is very disappointed to say the least."

Someone mentioned the GC building to her recently. *Jack.*

"I wanted to win this bid in Chicago for a more

personal reason." He squeezed her hand. "I really wanted to be here often to be closer to you."

So he could drop in uninvited and have her wait on him? Lizzie freed her hand from his grip. What the hell did Wallace want with her?

What did it matter what he wanted? She didn't have to settle for Wallace's scraps of attention. Jack's memorable kisses and the world of sensations they stirred inside her had opened her eyes to the possibilities. He might not want a lasting relationship with her, but he treated her with consideration, he desired her. She not only didn't have to settle, she wouldn't.

"I'm sorry, but I don't want to be closer to you, Wallace." Lizzie folded her arms across her chest. "I'd really like you to leave now."

"What are you saying?" He walked toward her closing the distance and held her by the backs of her arms, as if about to shake her.

Twisting sharply, she broke his hold and backed a few feet away toward the hallway in front of the kitchen leaving him by the stove at the far end of the narrow room. "You left for Europe without a word. I buried my parents without my fiancé at my side. You said you wanted to marry me. Do you have *any* idea how badly you hurt me?" Her breath came in gasps and her voice rose in fury.

Lizzie spied Marty skulking into the bedroom, tail between her legs.

"I already apologized for my behavior then. You're the one hurting me now. You and that Jack Clark." He stood straighter, his hand clutched against his midriff. "JP Hamilton takes great pleasure winning what is rightfully mine."

"What are you talking about? Who is JP Hamilton?"

"Clark's architectural firm." Wallace reared back and forth, laughing. "You didn't know. Maybe you should dig a little deeper into his motives for romancing you. He's obviously using you by hiding his relationship with my firm."

Confused and out of patience, Lizzie faced him, hands on her hips, "I've heard enough. I'm over you, Wallace. It's over. Please leave."

Gone were the array of benign expressions he'd plied to get in her door, poor forlorn, pained Wallace. Now a red blush rushed up his neck, over his cheeks and already thin lips tightened in a menacing line. She edged away as he rushed forward and pinned her against the wall. Trapped, this new person in front of her scared her.

"I'll tell you when it's over. There's no way Jack Clark is going to have it all." He yanked her arms over her head and crushed her lips with his.

Smothered, Lizzie fought to breathe, straining her neck muscles to break away from the invasion of his mouth as panic mounted and her heart beat erratically. She brought her knee up with force between his legs. He let her loose and doubled over, clutching himself.

She raced to the door, swung it wide and screamed, "Get out of here!"

Wallace slowly stood and glared at her with eyes that blazed with anger. "How dare you assault me, Elizabeth? It is *not* over." The anger in his eyes turned darker as he leered at her. "I will not permit him to use you against me."

"Get out." She stayed on the other side of the door in the outer hallway, hoping he wouldn't notice her shaking. No neighbor had responded to her shout, and she wouldn't go back into her apartment to attempt a call to security. She clamped her arms tight against her sides, her mind spinning out an exit strategy. If she could race inside the elevator first, she could push the alarm button.

Never taking those malicious eyes off her, he grabbed his coat and stalked forward, past her as if she were invisible.

As soon as he cleared the doorframe, she jumped back into the room and slammed the door shut. Panting, she leaned against the wall, exhausted from fright and confusion.

Wallace's motives for using her were unclear. And apparently Jack hadn't been honest either. Were both men setting her up as some sort of prize? No. After all, Charlie had arranged for Jack to go to her reunion with her. Charlie would never play games with her emotions. Would Jack? Why wasn't he upfront about knowing Wallace?

The telephone rang, and she let the call go to her answer machine. "Happy Thanksgiving, Beth." Jack's voice filled the room. She sucked in her breath. "I hope you have a nice day. Charlie tells me you're heading out tomorrow. I'll see you when you get back. I'll be missing you. Travel safe. Bye."

The tape stopped with a click. "Who are you, Jack Clark? And why should I believe you'll miss me?"

Chapter Sixteen

Jack missed Lizzie. She had been gone a little over a week, but it seemed longer to him. Everywhere he turned, he found reminders of her. The city streets he used to stride down unaware of his surroundings, now reminded him of walks with her. He wanted to stroll and think about her nestling close to him for warmth.

The number of times he sat back at his drafting table that week and thought of her sweetness surprised him because before meeting Lizzie he had always lost himself in his work.

He concentrated on pushing mental images of her aside. But it didn't work.

Even during the time-honored male ritual of watching Sunday football with Charlie, Beth sat beside him in his mind. It didn't help that his brother never shut up about her. And Jack found that he liked to listen to the superlatives Charlie attached to her.

Without a word about Beth during Jack's visits, her presence would still be felt in the brownstone. There were pictures of her everywhere.

Charlie's home was nothing like the musty dungeon it had been a few months ago. He had hired a housekeeper. Polished surfaces and immaculate floors gleamed. Open drapes let in sunlight or moonlight and a lemony smell permeated the air.

Framed photographs abounded in every room

downstairs. All of them included Mari and most also included Beth Moran. Jack didn't remember seeing them on mantels or on the piano when he had visited prior to Mari's death. But it was a big deal to Jack that Charlie now wanted ever-present reminders of Mari to surround him.

Thank God things had changed. There was even half-decent food to eat while watching Sunday games.

Jack couldn't banish the memory of Beth's excitement when he had watched the game with her or the creative insults she concocted for referees and rivals.

After work that day, he stopped by Lou's for takeout, and Rae spotted him at the counter.

"Hey handsome," she greeted him. "Where's your lady? Do you have a minute? I want you to sign something for me." She hurried, as much as her body would allow, to the back of the store.

Grinning, she thrust an eight by ten glossy into his hand. It was the photo Beth had taken of him and Rae together. "Beth brought this by the store a couple of weeks ago. Isn't it pretty? You've got to sign it for me, and I'm hanging it on the wall here. My manager gave me the OK. You are, after all, a famous architect."

Jack laughed but took the pen she handed him, when he realized she was serious. "I've never been asked for my autograph before."

He signed his name and handed the print back to her. "It's the first time, and I'm pretty sure the last time, too."

Inside the cab on the way home, he thought about Rae's reference to Beth as his lady. *His.* Jack didn't want to wait until the charity ball to see her again. He dialed her home number on his cell phone to leave her a message.

"Hey, Beth. It's Jack. Welcome home. I'm not sure when you're returning but if you can, please come with me for pizza on Saturday night. Or if you don't want pizza, we'll go anywhere you like. If you say yes, think of this as our first official date. I hope you say yes. Miss you."

Satisfied with the message, he pocketed his phone. He wanted a date with her. Maybe, by example, Charlie had turned the tables on Jack. You don't always have to hide in your house in a bathrobe to be cut off from living. Beth opened up something inside him that had been locked away too long. He was done with helping her get Wally back. The jerk would never deserve a woman like her. He wasn't sure he did either, but he wanted her for himself. He'd deal with what that meant later.

****

The Freedom Center project was going so well, Jack, always prepared to deal with inevitable snags in projects this size, didn't trust the good luck to last. The blueprints were approved and the myriad of permits issued in record-breaking time. He figured the mayor's office had a great deal to do with it.

Boston's highest official's clout had Jack perusing the lunch menu at the mayor's male members only club to discuss plans for the groundbreaking ceremony—instead of defending his plans to city bureaucrats as he supposed he'd be doing during this trip.

Jack enjoyed the one-on-one lunch and the mayor's genial disposition. Relaxing over coffee Jack spotted Wallace Prescott being seated with his party on the other side of the room. Engrossed in his own conversation, Prescott hadn't noticed Jack. The last thing Jack wanted to do was spar with Wally in front of the mayor.

*****

Wallace liked to room scan. It didn't take him long to spot Jack, although he did nothing about it at first. He watched Jack kowtow to the mayor.

Who does he think he is coming to my club and rubbing his success in my face? He thinks he can best me? Not in everything.

He waited until he saw Jack toss his napkin on the table before he excused himself from his table and crossed the room.

Jack was on his feet talking with the mayor when Wallace cleared his throat and tapped Jack on the shoulder to interrupt.

"Excuse me, Mister Mayor, but Clark and I are friendly competitors, aren't we Clark?" Prescott beamed in his honor's direction.

"That we are, Prescott." Jack shook Wallace's hand with a wry half-smile. "So, Wally, how's it hanging?"

Heat rose under Wallace's collar at the use of the abhorred nickname in front of the mayor of his city. But he wouldn't let this peacock get the best of him.

"Fine, fine. No need to ask you the same. I know things are going well for you. Last time I saw Elizabeth, I believe she mentioned as much."

I don't know what you are to her, Clark. But I'll teach her to injure me.

With a confidential air, he leaned toward the mayor, and locked eyes with Jack. "Clark and I have a mutual friend. Well, actually, she and I were much more than friends. Recently we've been reunited. About the same time I lost a couple of bids to your firm. Strange that you link up with my old girlfriend when we're in a bidding war, Clark. Don't you think that's strange, Mister Mayor?"

The politician regarded Wallace blankly, "If you say so." He turned his head toward Jack, "What is this all about, Jack?"

****

On high alert, Jack squinted at Wallace. What was this asshole trying to pull? "Yes, we do have a mutual friend."

"Indeed we do." Wallace chuckled, damned near a witch's cackle. "I have to watch what I say during pillow talk if we're ever bidding against each other again."

Jack's muscles strained, hands reflexively balled into fists itching to jab the smug bastard in the face. With effort, he relaxed his fingers. Mastering his reaction to this bombshell took all of Jack's self-control. Pillow talk? What the hell is that all about?

I'm out of here.

"We have an appointment. I'll give Beth your regards." He strode past Prescott and the mayor followed beside him.

But Wally pressed on. "Yes, indeed." He walked along with Jack and the mayor, positioning himself in the middle of the two men. "I think she might have mentioned you fondly while we were watching the parade together at her place on Thanksgiving Day. So adorable in her flannel pajamas."

Prescott raised his eyebrows and glared at Jack dead-eyed, daring him to pry loose the symbolic stake of male dominance he had just rammed home.

Beth was alone with Wallace in her condo? While he was missing her? In her pajamas? *What an ass I am.*

He kept a bland expression on his face as he tried to shake Prescott off. "That's nice to hear, Wally."

"Strange, though," Wallace continued. "She didn't know that we were competitors. Don't you think that's strange, JP?"

"Again." Jack emphasized the word so there was no mistaking the finality. "Good to see you."

The mayor kept pace with Jack's determined stride out of the room.

****

The encounter with Prescott was a lasting annoyance. Jack regretted the date invitation he had extended to Beth earlier in the week and almost cancelled it. As he had increasingly enjoyed Beth's company, he had forgotten her history with Wally. Stupid, but Jack had hoped he made her forget Prescott. Had Prescott accused him of being a shady businessman? It sure had sounded like it. That alone would disturb Jack, but even more disturbing was that Prescott made it sound like Beth was involved. As if Jack needed anybody's help in securing bids away from Prescott.

And she's sleeping with that shithead?

Although it was illogical, he was crushed that she chose to spend Thanksgiving with him and more appalled that she'd sleep with Prescott instead of with him. Made him regret any pangs of conscience he had suffered about following through on his attraction to her.

She had lied to Charlie about being too busy

packing to come to dinner, too. Apparently, she was busy all right. The more he thought about it, the more infuriated he became.

****

When Lizzie got home from her trip, she immediately checked her answering machine. She was actually starting to like the contraption. Punching the message button over and over going through the stream of recordings, she stopped when Jack's baritone voice delighted her. Even his voice triggered something mysterious and delicious inside her. No question, she was going to accept the date. She had a lot to ask Jack a.k.a. JP Hamilton.

Ever since Wallace insinuated that Jack had business motives for seeing her, she had done some deep thinking about time spent with Jack. She admitted that if he were guilty as charged, it was more for sins of omission than outright lies. She honestly couldn't remember his mentioning his profession, but she was sure he never discussed his competitive involvement with Wallace.

When she was with Jack, her head was muddled, first with nerves over seeing Wallace again, then with her own reaction to Jack's touch. Those slow, melting kisses and God, those muscles. Lizzie sighed. She'd figure out whether his interest in her was genuine, or if he was playing some kind of ego games with Wallace using her as his pawn. Dread that Jack was dishonest like Wallace weighed on her, a nauseating constriction in her stomach.

She called Jack's cell phone number and got his voicemail. "Hi, Jack. I'd love to go to dinner with you tomorrow night. I'll be running around all day. How about we meet at 7:30 at the Melting Pot on Dearborn? I'll make reservations. No need to call if this is okay. See you then. Bye."

Bet your ass, I'll go to dinner with you. I will not be lied to again.

****

Arriving at the restaurant a calculated fifteen minutes early, Lizzie wanted the luxury to sip some wine and nibble on an appetizer fondue while she waited for Jack. She had a lot of questions for him, but she didn't want to rush into an inquisition. She'd be calm and composed and rational, despite the fact that thoughts of Jack were ever irrational.

Unnerved when the hostess told her that her party was already seated, she followed her to the table where Jack was sitting. Was he glowering at her from across the room? Unblinking, Jack stared with no animation in his features whatsoever. No warm expression on his face to greet her, no sexy dimpling of his cheeks in a smile for her.

She strode to his table as she glowered right back at him.

****

Jack had been on slow simmer for days. Of course, Beth had a history with Prescott. Hell, he had aided and abetted the big reunion, hadn't he?

Then why was he so pissed she was in bed with the guy?

She looked terrific walking in his direction. The dim light in the restaurant seemed to shine only on her, playing on the highlights in her long brown hair and reflecting green sparks in her eyes. His nerve endings sizzled, and Jack still wanted to act on the attraction. He had never had a problem with casual sex or nonexclusive relationships. Hell, story of his life. But deep inside he knew he couldn't be casual with Beth or share her with the likes of Prescott…or any other man.

"Hello," she greeted him as she sat across from him.

He'd take it slow, be cool, and be logical.

He couldn't wait. "Why the hell did you lie to my brother about Thanksgiving?"

"Are you JP Hamilton?" Beth fired her question at the same time and he almost missed what she said.

Jack reacted first. "What? Of course not. JP Hamilton is the name of my company."

"What do you mean I lied to your brother? I did no such thing. Why didn't you tell me you're JP Hamilton?"

He grabbed the beer a waiter brought him and took a big swig out of the bottle before he set it on the table with a thud.

"Nicholas Hamilton was my grandfather. Before he died, he requested we change his firm's name to JP Clark Associates, and I balked. He wanted to leave the business to me, but I wanted to carry on his name. So, JP Hamilton it was. How many years have you known Charlie? I thought you knew all about my business. Why else would you have taken all those pictures of my buildings and sold Charlie on publishing them?"

She looked uncertain. "I thought you were a construction worker." She gulped her wine. "You designed those buildings? Why are *you* accusing *me* of lying?"

"Are you *slow?* Were you or were you not alone on Thanksgiving?"

"Slow?" She pitched toward him, her butt a few inches off the wooden booth and then plopped back down her eyes blazing.

Taking a sip of wine she repositioned the glass on the table with exaggerated care. "I had no idea you were the architect. All those years I've known Charlie, Mari hounded me to go out with you. I figured you were *slow* if you couldn't get your own dates."

Jack huffed, "I thought the same thing about you. You didn't answer my question. Were you alone on Thanksgiving like you told my brother?

"Yes. Well, no. First, yes, and then later, no. Why the hell didn't you tell me you're in competition with Wallace?" She sat back, lips pursed and rigid in her seat.

"I did...hell, maybe I told Charlie, what the hell difference does it make?"

This had to be one of the most frustrating conversations he'd ever had. "Why were you with Wally on Thanksgiving instead of me?"

A split second after he blurted out the question, Jack wished he could take it back.

****

She gaped at him. *He's jealous.* A thrill of pleasure shimmied up her spine. But, wait a minute.

"How do you know I was with Wally...I mean Wallace on Thanksgiving? I didn't plan it. He just showed up. I was in my pajamas watching the parade."

He arched one eyebrow and his eyes darkened. She almost laughed with sheer pleasure at how gorgeously riled she got him without trying. "They were an old baggy pair of flannels. Your Grandma Viv wears less to church on Sunday. You haven't answered my question,

Jack. How do you know I was with him?"

"I was in Boston on Monday working on ground breaking plans for The Freedom Center. I had lunch with the mayor, and Wally was with a group of men at the same restaurant. He wouldn't let me get out of the place before he told me what a great old time the two of you had on Thanksgiving Day."

"Wallace told you. Huh." She leaned back, the hard cool wood of the booth against her shoulders, stunned that Wallace would bring that horrible incident up.

"He also insinuated that I won the contract instead of him because of you."

"Well that's just ridiculous." Her mind spun trying to analyze Wallace's intentions.

"Of course it's ridiculous. But he threw this crap out to the mayor within earshot of who knows how many eavesdroppers at a power broker club. I have my reputation to think of."

"As I do mine," she retorted sharply. "I wouldn't hurt your reputation. Or Wallace's…"

****

"I get the picture." Her words stung. He guzzled the rest of the beer and asked for another, sitting across from her mute and unsociable like a married couple that had had one too many arguments and was only out together for the food. Not his idea of a Saturday night.

"Excuse me Jack, but I've developed a headache and I think I'll leave." She rubbed her temple with her right hand.

He was relieved that she was the first to say it. How could this go so terribly wrong? This was why he didn't get involved with women.

"No problem. Let me settle the bill, and I'll see you

home."

"No need." She moved to slide out of the booth.

Maybe he could make this right. Forget asshole Wally and his ego games. A light touch of his hand on her arm stopped her.

Beth looked deeply into his eyes. A jolt passed through him when he saw, reflected there, how his touch affected her. He couldn't deny that he was affected just as much.

"Ready to leave?" Jack gazed into the depths of emerald eyes.

"Yes," she whispered still moving away from him.

The current of desire shook him. In the cab, her nearness and her rose garden scent undid him. He reached for her like a man possessed and covered her mouth with his.

Her arms slid softly around his neck, and she leaned into the kiss, searching his mouth with her lips and tongue. Drawing apart to pretend some discretion, he could only sit, waiting until he could have more. Can't this car move any faster?

When the car stopped, he threw money over the seat to the cabbie and ushered her through the revolving door at her building.

Inside the elevator, her breasts pressed against his arm, and he shifted to pull her over, soft breasts against his chest as he jabbed the floor button and the doors closed. His hands swam under her coat and over her silky skin. His fingers teased under her sweater and skimmed smooth flesh and lacy underwear.

The pressure in his groin blanked his mind until he knew only the fierce need to taste her, take her. Locked together in a dizzying ascent that didn't stop when the elevator did, he lifted her into his arms and swept her to the door of her condo.

"I need to get my keys."

He kissed and nibbled her neck before he set her down. Shaking, she worked the lock and opened the door. Nudging her inside, he kicked the door closed and pressed her against the wall in the darkness, Marty skittering around his legs.

"Good girl, Marty." Beth reached down and scratched the dog's head, the friction from the movement driving him crazy. "Go play with your toys."

Jack let go of Beth long enough to pull off their coats and fling them on the floor. Hands gripped and stroked, digging under clothing, pushing it away, off, getting to the satin softness of her.

She sucked in her breath as his hands brushed over her breasts, then plunged inside her bra. Off, off, he wanted to feel her skin against his. When he practically ripped off her bra, he could see her pink nipples harden. He shed his shirt and bent his head to taste her.

Her breath caught and she whimpered, "No." Her body stiffened. He heard the soft sounds a woman makes when she cries.

He jerked his head up, did he hear right? He wasn't mistaken. Her eyes pooled with tears.

Jack forgot his own discomfort from being fully aroused. She didn't want this, didn't want him. Only Wally.

He picked up his shirt and put it on.

Dragging his hand through his hair, he uttered, "This was a mistake."

"Yes." She faced him and swiped her eyes with a fist.

Her cheeks flushed, her lipstick smeared and her hair all mussed, she looked sensational. It took a will of steel not to hold her in his arms and kiss the tears away. But he had never misunderstood the word "no" from a woman. Especially from this one, who obviously preferred pillow talk with only one man.

Her gaze never left his face. The short distance between them could have been miles. Mute, tears streaming, her eyes were wide with…panic?

He had never put that look on any woman's face and would never do it again.

"I won't bother you anymore."

She nodded. Didn't make a move to stop him.

"Goodbye." Appalled with his own behavior, he shrugged into his coat and left.

Chapter Seventeen

Jack. Lizzie thought of nothing else all week while she roamed the streets of New Orleans with a magazine reporter, documenting the gradual progress of the city's rebirth and the placement of evacuees after the holocaust of Hurricane Katrina.

Jack's mark would be on the new, New Orleans. Lizzie learned that a number of architects had donated their time and talents to rebuild the city since Katrina had ripped through and submerged it. JP Hamilton Associates led the pro bono effort. His JP Hamilton.

He'd left his mark on Lizzie, too. She didn't wonder anymore how his hands on her body might thrill her or where his kisses would take her, she knew. It was a terrifying place where every sensation was magnified until she thought she'd explode, lose herself irretrievably.

Now she regretted stopping him from making love to her and pushing him out of her life. The fact that she could stop him when his desire raged convinced her that he didn't want her for sex. She didn't know what he wanted.

Useless to think about him anyway. He hadn't called since he left her two weeks ago, half undressed and spinning. He never would.

"I won't bother you again." Jack, you're bothering me out of my mind.

Lately the scene of botched relationships with men, her peaceful little condo wasn't quite the haven it had once been for her. Men. She was through with Wallace and apparently Jack was through with her. If only she could have trusted Jack that night, not to use her, hurt her like Wallace had and would if she had let him back in her life. She ached to bring back that moment, immerse herself in what would surely be delicious sex with Jack.

But, what then? Tears welled and her vision clouded.

"I know," came a male voice.

She jumped at the reporter's gentle touch on her shoulder.

He looked at her, eyes full of compassion. "All this devastation is heart breaking, isn't it? But you have to give these people credit. There's a wonderful spirit here."

"Uh, yes. Yes there is." She composed herself and got back to work.

****

Lizzie primped for the charity ball on the night before Christmas Eve. The season excited her—a glittering time when the city was radiant with fairy lights, and the reflections of decorated buildings streaked the Chicago River in puddles of holiday colors.

The JPH Building, visible from Lizzie's living room, wore a necklace of red and green lights. She had always loved that building; in fact, had photographed it for the soon to be launched coffee table book, never knowing the man who was responsible for its creation.

When Charlie had called after she returned from

New Orleans to invite her to the event she had planned to go to with Jack, she had been flustered and confused. It had only taken a moment for her to realize that, of course, Jack had withdrawn his invitation.

Instead of crushing her, the turn of events challenged her. Helping Charlie had brought her and Jack together in the first place. Perhaps it would again. All the disturbing emotions she had experienced recently—like regret, nagging doubt, insecurity that sex was all men wanted from women thanks to Wallace—had crystallized into one certainty. She wanted Jack Clark.

After rubbing rose-scented lotion that contained little sparkles all over her body, she put on a lacy strapless bra and thong and slipped into a strapless gown of Christmas green velvet that skimmed the floor, draping her body softly and luxurious against her skin. She lined her eyes with emerald green and highlighted them with deep gray shadow for dramatic effect. The diamond butterfly choker that Charlie had given her was clasped around her neck, and she fastened her mother's diamond studs on her ears.

Charlie had given her Mari's diamond, tennis bracelet as an early Christmas present, and Lizzie wore that, too. She was comforted to take remembrances of her mom and her soul sister along with her for a special evening.

The look on Charlie's face when she greeted him at the door hit her target dead center. A good dose of male appreciation boosted her spirits.

"You look sensational, Lizzie girl. You'll be beating men off with a stick."

He looked handsome in a black tuxedo. Still slim,

but so much healthier, his dark blue eyes startled her, so much like Jack's.

Inhaling deeply to shake off the image, "You look wonderful, Charlie."

He produced a florist box from behind his back and gave it to her.

The corsage of white roses smelled heavenly, her favorite fragrance. She brought the roses near her face and breathed in the floral perfume. "Mmm. They're perfect, Charlie. Thank you." Stretching the band over her wrist, she kissed his cheek.

Outside he led her to a black Porsche, so highly polished she could see their reflections in its mirrored surface. He opened its door. She lifted the hem of her gown and tucked herself in the low seat.

"Whoa. Hot car. When did you buy a car, Charlie?"

"I didn't. It's Jack's."

He swung around the car and got in next to her.

"Won't he need it tonight?" Her spirits sank at the prospect that Jack wouldn't be there.

"Nope, he's already got a ride, so I asked if I could borrow the Porsche. It's got a lot of courage."

"I'll bet it does."

Charlie proved the statement as he gunned the car into the stream of traffic on Kinsey Street, then turned north on Clark. Like a kid on a carnival ride, she watched the blur of the car reflected in the storefront windows. She liked riding in Jack's car. It smelled like him and reminded Lizzie of him, too—midnight black handsome, sleek and powerful.

The location of the Performing Arts Building was obvious from blocks away. Huge Klieg lights threw crisscrossed beams into the icy black night. In front of the building, attendants opened the doors on either side of the car at the same time. She walked around to Charlie on the arm of the attendant. Charlie held out his arm to her, and she placed her hand in the fold of his elbow to walk together on a red carpet runner into the building.

The lobby had been transformed into a Christmas extravaganza. Dressed in evening gowns and tuxedos, all the other couples milled around in elegant pandemonium and looked like some super race of beautiful people. Everywhere silver garlands and wreaths of fresh pine trimmed with red velvet bows glittered with white lights.

In one corner of the lobby, a line formed along the side of a huge decorated Christmas tree donated by the former Marshall Field turned Macy's department store, to the dismay of Chicagoans who complained for months about the Field family selling out. A photographer took digital pictures of couples beneath the tree. An assistant worked the keys of a laptop with flying fingers. She printed, framed and handed photographs to each couple with a smile.

Charlie lifted two flutes of champagne from a waiter's tray and gave one to her.

"To Mari and a cure for this despicable disease." He clinked her glass.

She fingered the tiny butterfly at her neck. "To Mariposa with love. She would have adored this, Charlie."

He tucked her hand over his arm and moved her along with him. "Let's go get our picture taken for our place cards."

By his side, Lizzie strolled toward the tree. "Place cards?"

"Yep."

Closer to the tree, Lizzie appreciated its various sized butterfly ornaments, metal, silk, and stained glass, in a riot of colors.

"Oh, Charlie! These are gorgeous! Mari would flip over this tree."

In place in the line, Lizzie continued to admire the decorations.

"It was my idea. It's being raffled off tonight. Just about everything you see here is for sale, except for me and Jack." Charlie laughed. "We gave some thought to raffling ourselves off, too. You know, win a date with bachelor number one, or bachelor number two? But I'm not interested in a date, even for charity, and Jack refused claiming he's already taken."

He was so matter of fact with this information, that Lizzie almost missed it. "Taken?" Her heart skipped a beat.

Charlie looked at her curiously. "That's what he said. What do you think he meant by that?"

"I have no idea."

"Let's ask him."

Lizzie turned in the direction Charlie faced. Jack advanced toward them like a hunter, each muscle moving with grace. Then she noticed the stunning woman at his side. She was statuesque, easily five ten or more. Her hair was a cap of sable and auburn spikes. She wore a black fitted cocktail dress with spaghetti straps. The silky material molded to her body like it was sewn onto her curves and could barely contain her ample cleavage.

How had she forgotten how amazing Jack looked in a tuxedo? All man. With another woman on his arm. A lush woman that was Lizzie's polar opposite. She had never thought about Jack with another woman. How stupid. Even more stupid was the fact that she had been pining over a man she knew almost nothing about. Pretty naïve that she had presumed Jack meant her in his *already taken* remark.

The couple reached them and Jack circled his arm around the woman's waist. "Hello, Lizzie," his friendly tone drove home the implied *just friends* status with her.

Her heart fell when he didn't call her Beth, punctuating her fall from grace. She plastered on a smile.

Jack made the introduction, "Lizzie Moran, Gina Bianco."

Lizzie extended her hand to Gina, but was engulfed in a warm hug instead. A waft of earthy musk enveloped her.

Gina moved on to hug Charlie. A brilliant smile lit her perfect features. Mischief and eagerness danced in her amber eyes like the world was her playground.

The woman dripped sensuality. "Good to see you again, Charlie. This is a beautiful event. What is this line for?"

"Photos for place cards," Jack replied.

"Mind if we cut in?" Gina swished a hip, stepped in front of Lizzie and pulled Jack up to her with a tug of her French manicured hand.

Jack's arm brushed Lizzie's. He turned, met her eyes. For a moment Gina's presence evaporated along with any other woman in the room. Lizzie's heart lurched, but she didn't break eye contact. She could look for hours into his dark, magnetic eyes full of pure masculine confidence, dangerous and sexy as hell. A smile flickered in the corners of his lips, and then bloomed, while his eyes held hers conveying the intimate message that magnetism worked both ways.

Lizzie's lips curled in a slow smile. Men had wanted her before, but not the way Jack had. And in the depths of those navy blue eyes, she saw desire. He still wanted her. And she wanted him.

The line inched forward, and she broke eye contact with Jack. Jack and Gina stepped forward and followed the photographer's directions for their pose, turning toward each other while Lizzie trained an analytical eye on them. Gina's European flair complimented Jack's "black Irish" looks. They appeared to be at ease with each other.

But I make him uneasy.

Jack grabbed Gina's hand and walked away. Lizzie took her turn to stand in front of the tree with Charlie. The photographer directed them to stand on strips of tape on the floor. Charlie circled Lizzie's back with his arm. She leaned in to his side and rested her hand with the circle of delicate roses at her wrist on his arm.

A light bulb flashed. At a nearby table, Lizzie was handed a framed photograph.

She was delighted with the photo and Charlie's genuine smile.

"Charlie. Look at this engraving on the frame. It says '1st Annual Mariposa Arana-Clark Ball Benefiting Cancer Research.' And our names are on the bottom. 'Mr. Charles Clark escorting Ms. Elizabeth Moran.' What a wonderful keepsake. I love it."

"Told you, Lizzie. Place cards."

Hugging the frame possessively, she browsed the rows of silent auction tables skirted in crimson linen and draped with pine garland. Companies and individuals had donated every item imaginable to the silent auction. Bigger ticket items would be auctioned off after dinner.

Gleefully shopping for charity, Lizzie placed her bids for spa treatments, tickets to see *Wicked* and a box at a Cubs game. The item that she most wanted to win was the *Star of Hope* necklace commissioned by the American Cancer Society to pass from cancer survivors to prospective cancer survivors, and she couldn't resist bidding on a glitzy dog collar for Marty. She hoped that she'd win them all.

The vintage ballroom looked magnificent. White Christmas lights blended with candlelight and evergreens scented the air. Oak floors gleamed beneath the 19th century crystal chandeliers. Jack and Gina were seated at her table, and Lizzie was too wired to taste her food. As the dessert course was served, Jack left the table and walked to the center of the dance floor.

"Ladies and gentlemen." He waited a moment while the crowd quieted.

Lizzie couldn't stop the tears from streaming after hearing Jack and Charlie's speeches about Mari and her beautiful soul, especially as she watched Charlie's quiet tears.

Jack turned tears into laughter when he put on a straw, boater hat and brandished the cane a volunteer handed him. "Now ladies and gentlemen, prepare to part with some money." He pointed the cane at a screen that dropped from the ceiling.

By the end of the auction, Lizzie figured Jack had teased over a quarter of a million dollars out of wallets, bank accounts and credit cards. *The man is a charmer. But so much more. He may not want commitment, may be the worst man for me to get involved with, but who cares? He's a good brother to Charlie. Mari loved him, trusted him.* She vowed that if given another chance, she wouldn't resist Jack again.

When the dancing began, Lizzie itched to join in. Gina tugged Jack out to the dance floor and didn't sit out a song no matter what the band played. Lizzie watched them, envious and dispirited. No choice but to bide her time and see if there was an opportunity to ask Jack to dance.

Charlie sat next to her, legs angled straight in front of him. "You want to dance with Jack, Lizzie?" His quizzical expression dared her to deny it.

She laughed at her lack of subtlety. "Why yes, I believe I do. But I'm wrestling with how I'll go about that. Any suggestions?"

"Sure." He stood and held out his hand to her. "Follow me, little sister."

Gyrating to a Michael Jackson medley was great fun. Next up was *The Way You Look Tonight.*

"I *love* this song." She stood a foot away from Charlie and did an involuntary sway with the music. "It's the perfect song to dance with your partner."

Charlie opened his arms and winked. "We better get you over to him, then."

Lizzie stepped into Charlie's arms, heart pounding with anticipation. He held her loosely and led her smoothly in Jack and Gina's direction.

"Switch partners, bro," Charlie directed Jack, the

ring of the superior elder sibling in his voice.

****

The look on Beth's face packed so much earthy female power that it punched Jack below the waist. He wanted her right here, right now. Seduced, he passed a willing Gina over to Charlie, took Beth's hand and moved her into the circle of his arms. Her body molded to his. Dancing to this song—one of his favorites because it never failed to get a lady in the mood— petrified him with Beth. Every minute of the day since he had last seen her, all he thought about was seeing her again, which was a first. But he hadn't acted and had avoided calling her; afraid that with Beth there'd be no turning back.

"What a lovely evening this has been." Her warm smile beguiled him. "You and Charlie did such a good job."

"Thanks. I'm glad you're enjoying it." Even to himself, he sounded formal and forced. It unnerved him that he couldn't be easy-going, casual. Not to mention how aroused he was with the sweet rose-scented woman brushing against him. Her bare arms and shoulders gleamed in the dim light. Her breasts pressed against his chest. Why did she disarm him, haunt him despite the good sense of his decision to leave her to Wally and forget about her?

He looked down at her and met her gaze. Stars danced in her eyes from reflected light. The hall's noises receded into the background, the other dancers a blur of motion. Only Beth was clearly in focus as if locked in a private place with him.

"I won't see Wallace again, Jack. I've been wanting to tell you that." An expectant gleam in her wide green eyes, she grinned.

Was this an invitation?

Jack suppressed commenting, and regarded her passively. He was speechless with a surge of triumph that Wally was out of the picture. Her hopeful expression dissolved with her down-turned smile, "I like your lady, Gina. She's very nice."

He trumpeted a laugh. "Yes, she is very nice. But she's also very independent. She'd *hate* being referred to as my lady. We're friends."

She nestled her head on his chest, and the silken crown of her hair rested near his lips. A sigh ran through her, through him. His heart beat faster, just like the first night at the reunion when he'd held her in his arms. Then, she was fiercely loyal to a man who couldn't hope to deserve her. Since then Jack had begun to hope that she'd be fiercely loyal to him instead.

Beth raised her face again to reveal eyes glowing sultry and feline in the dim light. "Charlie told me you wouldn't do a date with a bachelor auction tonight because you're taken. Did you say that Jack?"

The dance ended, and he released her. She stood inches away all wide-eyed intensity and arched eyebrows, a perceptive female who'd wait all night for an answer.

Jack remembered the brief conversation with Charlie and the careless answer he'd given at the time with Beth in mind. He could easily have been referring to Gina and hadn't elaborated with Charlie. And wasn't about to elaborate with Beth, either.

"I don't remember. Let's go sit."

Jack turned away to dissuade her from pressing further. She followed close behind.

Back at the table Gina stood. "I need to get going, Jack, and we drove together." She smiled at him, a serene expression on her face. "I should have left sooner, but I've been enjoying myself. Are you ready to leave?"

Charlie popped up. "Can you drop me off on your way, Gina? I drove Jack's car tonight. Jack can take Lizzie home when the ball's over."

Charlie had the valet ticket in his outstretched hand.

"That's okay, Chuck." Jack did his best to flash a don't-go-there look at his brother. "I'll take Gina home."

"No, stay and enjoy yourself, Jacky," Gina cooed. She brushed Jack's arm with her hand, then stretched upward and pecked him on the lips.

Chapter Eighteen

"The music is beautiful, isn't it, Jack?"

"Uh." He tipped his head toward the band. "Yes. It's nice." His elbows on the table, he hunched over his beer glass, occasionally taking a swallow, apparently not in the mood to chat.

"I like this song. *What A Wonderful World.* Pretty."

"Sure. Pretty."

"Wanna dance?"

His gazed moved from the table setting to her eyes. She extended her arm to him across the table, palm up. Her hand hung empty for seconds, as he sat unmoving except for a narrowing of his penetrating eyes as she stared at him. He covered her hand with his, rose and walked her to the dance floor, wrapping his strong arms around her.

The music swelled inside her, coursing through her veins. Her heart beat with the rhythm of the drums, exciting, open to every sensation. She arched her neck, closed her eyes and parted her lips, inviting his kiss, hoping he'd accept. He kissed her.

Suspended, dreamlike, the only thing that kept her on the floor was the connection to his lips. The hammering of her heart drowned out the melody from the bandstand and the voices of others around her. As the music ended his lips left hers, but still, she stood with her eyes closed while the kiss went on further, longer in her mind.

Lizzie looked up at Jack watching her with a gentle smile. "More," she whispered.

A dare flashed in his penetrating gaze, and she met it, refusing to break eye contact.

He knitted his brow and his eyes darkened with an emotion she couldn't define. "You can't handle more."

The band played *Lady In Red.* "I disagree," Lizzie countered, grasping his hands in a dance pose. She nudged him so he'd take the lead in the slow dance.

"About what happened at your place..." His voice was barely above a whisper, his warm breath on the top of her head. "...I've meant to apologize. I won't lose control like that again."

"Oh yes you will. Tonight." Grinning at him, she thrilled at his stunned expression. She laid her head on his shoulder and pressed her body closer.

He was such a graceful dancer for a large man. She followed his lead with no effort. The flashes of heat at his touch turned into a constant current. The rush of sparks ran through her and inflamed her cheeks with pleasure.

"Come home with me." He whispered through her hair.

It wasn't a question. Even if it was, she could only say, "yes."

****

Unsure where she headed, Jack drove across the Wells Street Bridge, into the West Loop neighborhood. Wherever he was taking her, she was ready to trust him, and she wouldn't stop herself from doing that again. She had compared him and any other man who got too close to Wallace. What a farce where Jack was concerned. Wallace had never had her floating with just a kiss, never restrained himself from taking whatever he wanted no matter what she wanted.

Tonight she wanted to discover everything about Jack. No more misunderstandings or doubts. To be a guest in his home, in his personal space would be a wonderful exploration.

He pulled the car into the underground garage of a squat, red brick building that looked like a turn-of-the-century factory.

Jack inserted a key into the lock of double doors on the top floor of the building. Lizzie looked around and couldn't find any other doors on the floor. He opened the doors wide for her to pass in front of him.

The loft had windows covering every inch of exterior space, scarce interior walls boxed in the few rooms. Silvery metal ducts wound across the ceiling eighteen feet overhead. Inlaid dark cherry wood flooring sprawled beneath her feet. Automatically she kicked off her shoes not to mar its surface and padded further into the apartment, the floors warmed beneath her bare toes.

She touched a mahogany table, smooth and satiny beneath her fingertips and marveled at its beauty. A chaise lounge in copper colored leather looked like a molded "S," and a white leather sofa near the window had seat cushions that undulated in scalloped turns.

Lizzie glanced over her shoulder at Jack leaning against the double doors and found an amused smile on his face as he watched her inspect his place. She noticed the lighting came from the floor, when Jack twisted a knob to the right of the door that brightened the lights.

"That is so cool," she said, turning toward him. "I've never seen anything like this place anywhere."

"I doubt you will. I designed it all, and made most of it myself."

"Wow, Jack. I'm honestly blown away."

He dimmed the lights way down and walked to where she stood in the center of the huge living room. "You haven't been blown away quite yet."

His powerful arms drew her into a kiss, his soft full lips melding to hers, parting her lips. Her tongue tangled with his, exploring his mouth that tasted yeasty and sweet. Every thought in her head disintegrated like paper too close to a match. She arched toward him and pressed against the rock hard muscles beneath his tux. She wanted to explore every ridge of his body. No turning back. The thought never occurred to her, and she couldn't think anyway. Her body throbbed with need.

He kissed her neck and shoulders. The touch of his lips sent chills and scorching jolts through her at the same time. She reached behind her back and lowered the zipper of her gown with one quick jab. The soft green velvet slid down her body and pooled on the floor.

****

Jack stood back and looked at her in the dim light. Her fair skin gave off a light of its own. He touched the clasp of her bra and unhooked it with one, practiced movement. She shivered slightly but looked at him steadily, all brazen courage and enticing beyond words. He folded her into his arms, so small, so silky, so Beth.

Pushing his jacket down she helped him yank it off. Their fingers collided and tangled undoing the buttons of his shirt. Rid of the shirt, he clasped her to his chest, skin-to-skin. Her heartbeat was racing next to his as she wrapped her arms around his neck and pressed her lips to his. Taken. Taken by Elizabeth Moran.

Her tongue met his again, and he clung to her—sucked into a swirling, dizzying vortex. His body hardened and pulsed as her soft brushing against his erection drove him wild. He lifted her into his arms and cradled her body gently as he carried her to his bed.

Jack intended to caress and explore every tantalizing inch of her spread out below him. But she sat and unzipped his pants. She slid satiny fingers around him and stroked him into frenzy.

Beth took control. He couldn't stop her if he wanted to, no turning back. She pulled him down on the bed, straddled him and dealt with his clothes until he was naked beneath her. Bending her head toward his chest, she teased his nipple with her tongue.

His quick intake of breath must have encouraged her to do more, and she sucked lightly as his nipple hardened beneath her tongue. She trailed her tongue down his torso, her long hair brushing against his skin like a million soft feathers. Moving down his body she explored with hot breath and flicks of her tongue. He was powerless to do anything but enjoy every sensation. At fever pitch, he grabbed her and rolled to pin her beneath him.

Her body relaxed as she relinquished control. He put his hands and mouth on her breasts as her hips pitched erotically beneath his straddled legs. There was nothing but a lacy triangle of cloth between her and his straining erection. His mouth tasted her rose-scented skin as he laved his tongue between her breasts and pulled at the elastic of her thong with his teeth. He exposed the soft, secret flesh and explored it hungrily, ignoring her gasps until she stiffened and cried out with her release.

He didn't give her a chance to catch her breath, covering her mouth with his, varying the pressure of his lips on hers. She clung to him, arms wrapped around his shoulders, hands pressing the back of his neck, tongues tangled, moving together rhythmically. She reached for him, stroked him and moved him to where he could feel her heat and how much she wanted him. One thrust and she opened for him as if this were the hundredth time their bodies had joined, instead of the first.

Her hips thrust upward as he plunged deeper inside her. They were perfectly tuned to each other, driving up, up to that blinding place hanging suspended and breathless. Higher still for one piercing second, then a glorious freefall together.

She lay sated and loose-limbed in the arc of his arms with her head resting on his chest. "My God, Jack." She exhaled. "Oh, my God."

"Are you okay? Beth, did I hurt you?" He pulled her on top of him with one powerful sweep so he could see her face.

"Oh, no." Her eyes alight, her smile reassured him. "I have no words for how wonderful that was."

He laughed and nuzzled her neck. "Not bad for the first time," he said, suddenly okay that there was no turning back with her.

"We'll do better the next time as we get to know each other's bodies better."

She propped herself over his chest and looked at

him with disbelief. "What in the world is left to learn? I'm pretty sure you covered all of my, uh, territory."

****

Jack rolled her back on the bed and pinned her arms over her head setting her aflame again. He reached above her head, took each of her fingers into his mouth in turn, sucking and pulling gently against her flesh.

Lizzie closed her eyes and let him play with her. Her hips moved toward his body and her breathing became shallow in mounting arousal.

"Let's see if I'm right and the next time is better." He didn't wait for her agreement.

She spent the night in Jack's bed, much like she had spent every night since she met him, sleepless and yearning. But tonight, she yearned for more of the delights of making love with him, and she lacked for sleep because those yearnings were finally fulfilled. Sometime in the early morning hours of Christmas Eve she drifted off, waking with a start when sun streamed over her shoulder. She lay on her side, facing a closet door.

Lizzie knew where she was in the strangely silent room. Left alone. Like Wallace left her. She turned, fearful, toward the window and braced to find Jack missing beside her.

He slept, his face beautiful and peaceful with his legs splayed, his black hair curled against the white pillowcase and his chest uncovered. She brushed her fingers in his soft, black chest hair and marveled that this was the way she was starting her Christmas Eve day.

"Greedy, are we?" He opened one eye.

She had disturbed a hibernating bear. He may be

sleepy, but he could rear up any minute. What the heck, she'd play with fire. She plunged her hand beneath the covers and got his full attention.

He lifted her on top of him and the heat built fast. She straddled him, guiding him inside her. A piercing climax came at the same time he groaned and released. Lizzie slid softly down to the reality of the cocoon of his arms, and smiled tenderly at him. "I love you, Jack."

He searched her eyes as if to make sure he had heard right, and when she didn't take the statement back in word or in gesture, he kissed her long and hard. Then he whispered, "I love you, too."

****

Lizzie couldn't stop smiling all the way home. Suffering aches and twinges as she slid into the cab, she didn't mind the soreness—like taking a reminder of the glory of being in Jack's arms wherever she went.

He was such a gentle, giving lover as if it were her first time. In a way, making love to him was her first time, and her second, and third. Jack was amazing. Nothing that had happened with Wallace could compare. She had experienced the sacred mystery of cosmic sex. With Wallace she had been little more than a receptacle. With Jack she was a partner who got as much as she gave. Wallace had sex. Jack made love with her.

She daydreamed about being with Jack again later for a quiet, intimate Christmas Eve celebration. She heard the phone ringing as she unlocked her door.

She expected to hear Jack's voice when she answered it, so it took her a moment to realize that it wasn't him on the line.

Chapter Nineteen

"Mick, what? What? Mick, please slow down. I can't understand you."

"Liz you have to come. I'm losing her." Mick sobbed into the phone.

"Mick, please. Tell me what's happening!"

He took a deep, shaky breath like wind in her ear. "The hospital called. Kay started hemorrhaging. I got here as soon as I could, but I didn't get a chance to see her before she went into emergency surgery. Oh God, Lizzie, I should have stayed overnight with her. She's still in the operating room, and no one has told me anything. Lizzie, I had to decide whether to save my wife or my babies if it came to that. God, help me…" His cries for help tore her open.

He gasped and choked out the rest. "God forgive me, but I chose Kay. I can't live without her. But I can't lose our children, either."

He broke down again. "Please, Liz, can you come? We need you. I don't know what I will do if anything happens to her."

"You're not going to lose anybody." *Please God, let me be right. Watch over Kay and her little ones.*

"I'm on my way. I'll be there as soon as I can. Let me call the airlines, and I'll call you back to let you know when. Is anyone else there with you?"

"Our families are on their way."

"Okay, hang in there. Kay will be just fine."

"Thanks."

Lizzie's heart rate accelerated as she tried to overcome panic and take action.

Dear God it's Christmas Eve. Please, please, please let me find a way to her. She hoisted the heavy Chicago Yellow Pages directory off the shelf of her kitchen cabinet, but before she had a chance to locate any airlines numbers her phone rang.

"Elizabeth. It is Wallace."

Shit. "I don't want to talk to you, goodbye."

"Wait!" The phone was three inches from her ear already, but his yell got her attention.

"What? I have no time to talk," she yelled into the phone.

"I know. I was at Mother's when she got the call from Kay's mom. I know you well enough to know you would be moving heaven and earth to get to Boston. Trying to get a flight on Christmas Eve will be impossible."

"I know, but I have to try. Goodbye."

"Go to Midway Airport. There is a chartered plane waiting for you."

"What?"

"I called and chartered a plane for you. It is waiting. Hurry."

Relief coursed through her, and she let out a rush of air realizing she had been holding her breath for the past few minutes.

"I don't know why you did this, but thank you." Then her adrenaline kicked in again. She had to move. "I've got to go."

"No thanks needed. I do care for you, Elizabeth.

Get to the airport. Kay needs you."

Lizzie needed to stay connected with Mick, so she dialed his cell phone number as soon as the cab started rolling. There was nothing new he could tell her, but just hearing his voice helped her to stay grounded. He seemed calmer, but she fell apart after she hung up. Trembling all over, tears fell unchecked; she could easily slip into hysteria. Brushing the tears away with the back of her hand, she forced some control over her emotions. Mick needed her to be strong. Kay needed her to help him.

Settled in a cushioned, captain's chair on the most luxurious plane she had ever seen, she dialed Mick's cell again. Her third time. She told him she was on her way and that she would see him soon. A quick disconnection from Mick's line, and then she dialed Jack's phone. Jack. Just thinking his name was like being wrapped in a blanket to keep out this terrible, cold fear. It seemed like a long time since he had held her in his strong arms. The battery in her cell phone started to beep the 'low bat' signal. Just as his recording sounded, it died.

"Damn thing!" She threw the useless phone in her purse, longing to hear Jack's voice. No choice but to wait and call him from the hospital because she didn't remember to bring her charger with her.

Feeling like a rock star, she disembarked the plane when it came to its berth at Logan Airport, and climbed into a limo parked at the foot of the stairs. The car whisked her directly to Mass General.

****

Jack walked up the circular driveway in front of Beth's building. Balancing two *Starbucks* cups on a cardboard tray, he swung a bag of scones whistling as he walked, not a care in the world because Beth loved him.

The words had resonated deep inside him, and he knew he loved her, too. He had never said those words to a woman before and was still amazed that he had. His world was bigger somehow, brighter. He didn't think that he had it in him to love a woman exclusively and believe that she'd be faithful to him.

Jack had never understood why it was so hard for his dad and Charlie to go on with life after the loss of their wives. Now he understood how a man was helpless to do anything else but love his woman. His Beth.

In such a short time, she had become part of him, necessary as every breath. Loving her was worth the risk of losing her. He wanted her with him today and every day. Since he couldn't wait until tonight to see her, an impromptu coffee delivery got him to her building.

Jack pushed through the revolving door as a little girl walked through the other side with a dog on the leash she held. Recognizing the little, wiggling terrier on the other end of the leash, he continued to follow the door around back outside.

"Excuse me. Isn't that Marty?"

The little girl held the leash tighter. But Marty reacted to Jack's voice. She wagged her nub tail, plopped down on the grass and offered her pink belly for a scratch.

"Marty knows me. I'm a friend of Miss Moran."

"You know Lizzie?" The girl still looked wary. She started to inch back toward the door.

Darla, ever watchful inside, came out from behind the counter and through the revolving door.

"Mr. Clark, hello."

"Hello, Darla. How are you today? I was just saying hi to Marty. Is Beth home?"

The little girl's gaze darted back and forth between them.

"No, sir. She left in quite a hurry," Darla advised him. "She had me call a cab for her, and she left over two hours ago."

The little girl piped up. "She is going to be an aunt. She left for the hospital. She doesn't know when she will be back, so I am going to take care of Marty for her."

Jack crouched down and looked at the young girl at her eye level. "Well, that is a big responsibility."

"My mom is helping me." Marty pulled the girl closer as she tried to get pets from Jack.

"I'm sure Beth really appreciates the help."

Jack waved goodbye as Marty tugged the little girl toward a walk.

Concern for Kay—since Beth had left in a hurry—had him calling his secretary at home. Even on Christmas Eve she assured him that everything would be ready for him when he arrived at the airport. What would he do without Eileen? Her salary would be making a nice jump in the New Year. He hailed a cab and headed to O'Hare airport knowing that by the time he got there, Eileen would have everything lined up.

His prepaid First Class ticket in hand, he waited fifteen minutes at the gate for his Boston-bound flight to board. Within an hour from leaving her building, he was on his way to meet Beth. He wondered why she hadn't called to tell him the news. Probably forgot her phone again. Worry pinched him. *Please take care of Kay.*

****

Lizzie ran through the hallways of the hospital to the bank of elevators. When the doors opened on the third floor, she rushed to the ob-gyn waiting room. Mick was slouched in a chair with his head in his hands on the other side of a glass window. His family surrounded him.

Her heart turned to ice. Bracing herself for bad news she shoved through the door. Mick saw her, jumped to his feet and enveloped her in a bear hug. She cried and trembled like him.

Clinging to him, Lizzie's heart broke.

"It's okay, Lizzie girl. Don't cry. She's going to be okay. You just missed the doctor. She's going to pull through. It was touch and go, but she's strong."

"What about the babies?"

"Oh my God! I'm a daddy! You're an aunt! We have two daughters. Noel Elizabeth and Merry Katherine came into the world about a half hour ago. I was with her during the C-section. Wait until you see them. Perfect. Two little Kays. I might be a little biased, but they are the most beautiful babies ever born."

"Noel Elizabeth."

"Yep, she's named after her godmother."

Lizzie's tears rained down her cheeks. Her legs weakened, nearly buckled under her.

She heaved a relieved breath. "Noel and Merry. Born on Christmas Eve. The perfect Christmas presents. What happened? What about the hemorrhaging?"

A man in scrubs, bags under his eyes, came into the waiting room. "Mr. Lynch, your wife is being taken to her room now. Wait a few minutes, and then she can have visitors."

"Thank you, doctor." Mick pumped his hand. "I can't thank you enough. Merry Christmas."

"You're welcome. Your daughters are in the nursery if you would like to show them off to their new family. Enjoy your double blessings." The doctor's gaze moved from Mick's face to the family who listened with rapt attention. "Merry Christmas to all of you."

Lizzie waited her turn to visit Kay. After the family had gone in, two at a time, Mick entered the waiting room and took her hand. "Come on Auntie Liz, Kay is asking for you."

Shocked at how pale and fragile Kay appeared against the stark, white hospital sheets, she forced a cheery smile. Kay's lips were blue, and she trembled under a pile of blankets.

Mick gave Lizzie's hand an assuring squeeze. "The nurse told me the shakes and that bluish color are reactions to the anesthesia." He nudged her toward the bed.

"Hey, Momma." Lizzie reached toward Kay's hands.

"Bella. So glad." Kay's ice-cold hand clasped Lizzie's damp one. "Have you seen my girls?"

"No, I was waiting to see their momma first. Damn, you gave me a scare."

"Scared, too, but so worth it," Kay's voice raspy, her speech slurry. "Poor Mick. My girls are so beautiful." She burst into tears.

"What is it? Is something wrong? Are you in pain? Do you want me to get a nurse? Don't cry."

"Crazy. It's OK. Happy tears."

Lizzie squeezed Kay's hand, tears welling. "I thought you might be looking for sympathy. This is a pretty lame way to get chocolate, if you ask me. Not this time. If anyone deserves chocolate this time, it's me. Here I am at the birth of my nieces, and I was in such a rush to get here that I left my camera bag behind." Her fear subsided and her heartbeat slowed down when Kay gently squeezed her hand back.

"I, the official photographer of this family, have to go to the hospital gift shop and purchase a disposable camera. Do you have any idea how embarrassing that will be for me? A lousy plastic camera is all I'll have to photograph two of the world's most important children. So, missy, it's payback time. You owe me a giant box of Russell Stover. You're too deprived in Boston without Fannie May." She hoped humor would help Kay forget her pain as it helped Lizzie forget that she'd almost lost the only family she had. She couldn't lose them again.

Kay laughed, more like a strangled chuckle. Her friend clutched her belly and winced but chuckled anyway. Lizzie leaned down and hugged her around IV tubes and buzzing machines. She didn't want to let go.

"I don't know what I would have done if anything happened to you." The mere thought terrorized her.

Lizzie locked her gaze with Kay's, and all that was between them spilled out in combined tears and laughter.

Mick chose that moment to come back into the room. "Oh boy. What's going on here?"

"Get used to all the hormones, daddy. You're outnumbered now." Kay's eyes shone.

Mick grinned, a look of pure adoration for Kay on his face.

Lizzie sensed their need to be alone. "I'll be right outside, sweetie. Get some sleep. You're both going to need it. It's time that I made silly faces at Merry and Noel through the nursery window."

She was exhausted, her feet like lead. Fear had a way of draining everything.

I have to call Jack.

Missing him sorely she wanted to be in his arms again and have what Kay and Mick have. She wanted children. *Beth wants it all.*

Closing the door behind her, Lizzie debated if she should see the twins or hunt down a phone. She walked toward the nursery scanning overhead signs hoping she'd find a payphone on the way.

Kay and Mick's families clustered around the glass window and made appreciative noises at the babies' every move. Wallace stood in the middle of the group, like a cactus in a flower garden, looking ill at ease. He gave her a hapless, crooked smile.

God, what is he doing here?

She forced a smile and approached the group.

Peering through the nursery window, she spied the twins and couldn't help but grin.

Apparently she inadvertently encouraged Wallace to pipe up, "I'm not exactly in my comfort zone. This is not where I planned on spending Christmas Eve."

"I'm sure Kay doesn't expect you to be here," Lizzie remarked through clenched teeth hoping he'd get the hint.

"Elizabeth…"

Lizzie cut him off, "I have to find a phone."

"Going to call Jack Clark?" He sneered.

Lizzie rolled her eyes. "None of your business." She stepped away from the window and surveyed the hall for a likely place for a payphone.

"Here use mine." He strode over to her and handed her his BlackBerry.

"You can't use cell phones in the hospital." Lizzie held the phone toward him to return it.

"You can use it in that waiting room. I did and no one tried to stop me."

Rules don't apply to you, do they Wallace? Anxious to connect with Jack she'd give Wallace some cash for the call. "OK, thanks. I'll be right back."

****

"Here you go." Wallace accepted his phone from Elizabeth and shoved it in his coat pocket.

"Where did the family go?" She looked down the empty hallway.

"To Kay's room I think."

"OK. Take care, Wallace." She turned her back on him and walked toward the elevator bank.

"Just a minute, Elizabeth. Aren't you going to thank me for arranging your flight?"

Turning around, she advanced toward him, pursing her lips into a thin line. "Why did you?"

"An olive branch, Elizabeth. Have you forgotten how generous I am?"

"Why *yes I have,*" she replied with an insulting sarcastic tone in her voice.

He huffed. "You obviously don't deserve my generosity."

Hands on her hips she frowned. "How much do I owe you? I'll write you a check now."

The elevator doors behind her slid open. Jack Clark stood inside, head bent downward.

Wallace grabbed Elizabeth by the arms, yanked her toward him and plastered his mouth on hers, his arms locking her against his chest. He arched his back lifting her feet off the floor while he continued to glue his lips to hers, spearing his tongue into her mouth.

Out of the corner of his eye he saw Clark staring at them, and with the fierce pressure of his lips, Wallace squelched any sounds from Elizabeth except a faint mewl that he hoped Clark wouldn't hear.

The elevator doors swished closed, and he dropped her back on her feet.

"You son of a bitch!" Nearly toppling over as she shoved his chest with both hands, he staggered a few steps backward.

She dragged the back of her hand across her lips, eyes blazing. "Don't you *ever* touch me again!"

Knuckles on each hip she leaned forward, shoulders heaving. She raised her head, and stared at him, disgusted. "How dare you treat me like this? I don't owe you a thing, Wallace. To think I once loved you, wanted to marry you."

Wallace brushed past her and punched the elevator button. Pivoting, he turned into the swing of her arm, the stinging slap landed squarely on the side of his face. He grimaced but would not stoop to hit a woman, in public anyway.

"Return my $10,000 donation check," he growled.

The bell sounded and the elevator opened. He stepped inside and pushed the ground floor button staring at her. "I never intended to marry you, by the way."

Chapter Twenty

Convinced he was an idiot, Jack kicked the door to his closet shut with the toe of his boot. The slam echoed through the silent house.

Whenever he had closed his eyes in the uncomfortable, plastic, airport chairs or the more comfortable seat in First Class, he saw Lizzie and Wallace locked together like lovers.

He figured Liz and Wally'd had a good laugh at his expense. Duped by her innocent act. She had always wanted Wally first.

What the hell happened? For years he guarded himself and avoided the pain he'd seen in his father's eyes every day growing up. He had let his guard down for one solitary night and look where it left him. He didn't want to look in the mirror and see Dad's pained expression on his face.

Emptying his pockets onto the glass end table he picked up one item. No need to open the box knowing what was nestled inside on a bed of black velvet. He had taken the ring out and tested its brilliance in the overhead light on the plane heading to Boston, and he'd left it in his pocket on the flight home. What the hell had he been thinking?

His grandmother had been surprised, but so pleased, when he showed up at her door Christmas Eve morning.

Was it really only yesterday? Yeah, it was. Merry Christmas, Jack.

He kicked the closet again. It seemed like a lifetime ago.

Thrilled to give him the diamond that her mother had worn, Grandma Viv had turned the ring over to him without asking one question. The ring had been promised to him when he found his special love. Yesterday, he thought he had found his soul mate.

At least he had seen Lizzie's true colors before he made a complete fool of himself.

Now he would have to explain to Grandma Viv that it was a false alarm, a crazy mistake.

A primitive anger built in his chest. He wanted to smash his fist into the wall. How had she manipulated herself into his life? For years his anger with his father for falling apart when Mom left seemed justified. Like father like son. As much as he hated to admit it, he had been tough on his father. This kind of loss could rip a man in two.

But he'd be stronger than his father, wouldn't crumble or fall apart. He refused to wallow in the pain.

The message alert buzzed on his cell phone. He had avoided retrieving his messages since he left Boston. Giving in, he went through the motions of dialing into his voicemail and listened. When he heard her voice, he damned himself for not being able to hang up.

"Jack, hi, it's Lizzie…Beth. I can't wait to talk to you. And hear your voice. I have the most wonderful news. Kay had the babies. Noel Elizabeth and Merry Katherine." Her infectious laughter bubbled in his ear.

"They're going to get even for those names one

day. I didn't get a chance to call you. Everything was so crazy. Mick called, and Kay was hemorrhaging, so I had to get here as fast as I could. I just ran out the door. Even forgot my cameras. Can you believe it? No cameras to take pictures of the prettiest babies ever born. Then my cell phone died. Didn't do me any good that I finally remembered the damn thing. Too bad I forgot the charger. It was touch and go with Kay, but I've seen her and the doctor says she's going to be all right. I just came from seeing the girls. Beautiful, amazing, angels. Wow I am going on and on and Merry…"

The timer cut her off before she finished her message. He hated the fact that he missed her. She sounded so sweet, so genuine.

He hit the return call button needing to talk to her. Maybe she could convince him he hadn't seen what he thought.

"You have reached Wallace Prescott. I am unavailable. Leave a message."

Jack threw the phone across the room and sagged onto his bed. He had his answer.

She's with him. But why?

He pulled the pillow from under the bedspread, buried his face in it and was assaulted with the delicate scent of Beth's perfume. The smell of roses clung to his sheets and his hands. Thoughts of their passionate lovemaking jolted him off the bed. Tearing the sheets off, he bundled them up and threw them in the hamper.

Jack couldn't close his eyes in his own bed without seeing her poised beneath him naked, taunting him. He grabbed a duffle bag from his closet, threw a few things in it, zipped it up, tugged the strap over his shoulder and headed out of the bedroom. In the kitchen, he noticed the light flashing on the answering machine. He deleted all the messages without listening to any of them. Out into the cold, he jumped into his car and screeched out of the driveway.

He knew exactly where he would spend the holidays and would call Charlie on the way to apologize for not being at Christmas dinner with the family. A pang of guilt assaulted him over leaving Charlie alone on this first Christmas without Mari, but he was in no state of mind to offer comfort to his brother. No need to explain his change of plans. He would just tell him something came up. Charlie could think what he wanted to think. He couldn't explain why. At least not yet. Maybe never.

****

Early Christmas morning Lizzie walked into Kay's hospital room with a put-on smile. She was sure her red-rimmed eyes gave her away.

"Merry Christmas." Lizzie knew her voice sounded weak and wavered.

"Merry Christmas, Bella. Wow, you look worse than I feel. Mickey, darling, can you let Lizzie and I have some girl time?" She kissed her husband and gave him a beatific smile.

When he closed the door behind him, Kay gazed at her shrewdly, her eyes narrowed to slits. "What's up, Bella?"

Lizzie fidgeted with her hands unwilling to meet Kay's eyes. "I don't know what to do. I've left messages everywhere for Jack, and he didn't call me back. I've left messages with Charlie, and he didn't call me back. Why does this keep happening to me?"

"Well what's the big deal? It's Christmas. Maybe he's busy with family." Her casual words pained Lizzie.

She frowned. "I'm so afraid that the same thing has happened to me with Jack as with Wallace. It appears Jack doesn't want anything to do with me."

Even though she didn't think she had any tears left to cry, Lizzie's eyes welled again as she sank down to sit on the foot of Kay's bed.

Kay's eyes widened. "Oh, my God. I understand now. You slept with Jack, didn't you?"

"I thought I made love with Jack." Lizzie swiped under each eye with the knuckle of her index finger.

"Spill it. I want the facts. Where? When? How?"

"We can talk later, you must be exhausted," she said, hardly in the mood to provide details.

Lizzie stood poised to approach Kay for a hug and then leave.

Kay's eyes softened. "I'm not tired. Don't you want to get this off your chest?"

Lizzie paced around the small room. "I went back to his house after the ball. It was wonderful, heavenly, amazing. I told him that I loved him." Despite her fear that Jack had deserted her, she was glad to share this confidence with Kay. Just twenty-four hours before, the memory of that evening was joyful.

"What did he say? Did he tell you he loved you, too?"

"Yes. But obviously he didn't mean it." Tears tracked down her cheeks again.

"Honey, you are a beautiful, strong, caring, lovable woman. No man you want could resist you, least of all Jack. Are you sure he's avoiding your phone calls? Maybe he hasn't even gotten them. There has to be some kind of mistake. Something isn't right here. Jack would never hurt you. I saw the way he looked at you at the reunion."

"I will *not* cry about this anymore." Lizzie looped around Kay's bed, aimlessly pacing. "Hard to believe that Wallace might be right about something."

"What in God's name does Wallace have to do with any of this?"

Kay reclined against her pillow, arms folded over her stomach, watching her movements keenly.

"It's a long story, but the two of them are competitors. Wallace claims there's some sort of ego game going on between the two of them." Lizzie sat on the bottom of Kay's bed. "Wallace can go to hell. And if Jack's playing games, he can go right with him."

"Oh, Wallace has a screw loose. If anyone has ego problems, it's Wallace. You can't trust him."

"Damn straight."

Kay raised her eyebrows. "That's the spirit."

"You know what that son of a bitch did?"

"Which son of a bitch are you referring to?" Kay gave her an impish grin.

Lizzie snorted a laugh. "Last night, outside the nursery, he practically muzzled me with a kiss. Kissed me so hard that I could barely breathe. Tried the same thing in Chicago on Thanksgiving. I was honestly afraid I wouldn't be able to stop him."

"I hope you kicked him to the wall." Kay punched her hand with her fist.

"I kneed him in the groin in Chicago."

Kay cracked up, contagious for Lizzie.

"Stop," Lizzie protested, sinking back down of the end of the bed again, tears streaming down her cheeks, this time from laughing so hard. "I left a couple of bruises on his chest last night. I believe I screamed don't ever touch me again. Slapped him the face, too. He wants his donation check back. And his nasty final remark in the elevator was that he never intended to marry me."

"Screw him."

"Kay, I swear." Lizzie held up a hand that shook with her giggles. "You're going to make me wet my pants."

"Good riddance to Wallace. Don't give up on Jack. I'm usually a good judge of character."

"Then why hasn't he called me back? I bought a new charger and I didn't turn the phone off all night. I left a message on Charlie's machine, too. Doesn't anybody answer phones anymore? I just wish someone would call me back."

"Oh honey. Don't jump to conclusions. Who knows? Maybe Jack's on his way here to surprise you."

"I hadn't thought about that." *Wouldn't that be nice?*

"Sorry to interrupt." Mick poked his head in the door. "I just wanted you to know that the family has arrived, *all* the family." He rolled his eyes. "They're about to barge in here to sing carols to you, Kay. Thought you'd appreciate a warning."

"Thanks, honey."

Lizzie held Kay's hands. "I'll be in the way here. I have to get going."

"Where are you going? It's Christmas. Stay here and celebrate with our wacky families. You're never in the way. You're my family, too."

"I'll stay a few days, I promise. I think I'll check in

226

at The Charles instead of the motel down the street. Pamper myself a little. Merry Christmas, Kay."

Tears brimmed in Kay's eyes. "Lizzie, I don't want you to be alone. Are you sure you should go?"

Lizzie scooted off the end of the bed and rushed to Kay's side, stooping over for a hug. "Ah, don't cry, honey. I'll be fine. I always am."

Twenty people crowded into Kay's room bellowing *White Christmas*. The eggnog or mimosas must have been a little too strong at brunch because the singing was off-key and off-tempo by a lot. Lizzie blew Kay a kiss from the door and left the ward, stopping briefly to peek at the twins in the nursery.

She had a dull ache in the center of her chest as she walked out of the hospital. She didn't want pity from Kay or her family. Although she knew she was welcome, she would rather be alone.

Even after all these years, she couldn't be with another family on Christmas, no matter how close. She would come back tomorrow and spend a few days with Kay like she had done the summer after she lost her parents and take the time away from Chicago to lick her wounds. Maybe Kay was right. Maybe Jack would surprise her.

****

Seated on the bed in her room, she picked up her phone and dialed. Pick up, Jack. Prove me wrong. Prove you can handle a relationship.

She got his recorded invitation to leave a message. Sighing, she'd do this once more, "Hi. It's me again. I haven't heard from you yet and I thought you might wonder where you could reach me. I'm at The Charles. Hard to believe there's a room available on short notice it being Christmas and all, but I'm in suite 317. I'm sure you have the hotel number, so give me a call when you get this message. I miss you Jack."

She placed the phone in its cradle, lay on the bed, pulled her legs up to her chest in a fetal position and cried herself to sleep.

****

Two days later Lizzie had given up any hope that Jack was going to show up and surprise her. In an attempt to keep some of her dignity intact, she had, so far, resisted the temptation to call Jack again. But the urge nagged her every waking moment, and even in her dreams. She couldn't, wouldn't embrace the idea that he had abandoned her, too.

Did all men only want conquests and when they got what they wanted move on?

The Christmas holiday over, he'd be back to work. In one final attempt to reach him, she dialed his office number and identified herself to the woman who answered.

A pleasant silky voice, "Miss Moran, Mr. Clark is not in the office this week. If you would like to leave a message, I'll be sure he receives it when he calls in."

"He's calling in? That's wonderful. Thank you. Please just tell him that I called and need to speak with him."

The hotel phone rang a few moments later and shattered the funereal silence of her room. She dove across the bed and grabbed it on the first ring.

"Liz. Finally. Can you tell me what the hell is going on? My answering machine tape is full of messages from you and Jack. I've been trying to call both of you."

Jack could call Charlie and not her?

"That's funny," Lizzie glanced at her cell phone on the bedside table plugged into the charger. "My phone's charged."

"I've been calling the house. I finally took a chance and called Kay. And she told me you were staying at The Charles. Is Jack there with you?"

Her heart seized, alarmed. "No, he's not here. You don't know where he is, either? I've left messages everywhere for days and he hasn't called me back. Charlie, what's going on with him?"

****

Charlie heard the anguish in her voice. If he had his brother in front of him, he would strangle him. *What has Jack done to my precious Lizzie?*

"He's at Pop's cabin, and he's fine. I have no idea what's going on with him."

"What cabin? Is there electricity there, cell towers?" Liz screeched.

"Very sophisticated. He's called me several times lately. Let me worry about him. I'll figure it out," he promised her. "When are you coming back? I need you here to do press for the book launch."

She answered in a monotone, "I'm not coming back for a while."

How did this all go to shit? He was positive he had gotten them together the night of the ball. All the reasons Lizzie was instrumental to this book launch ran through Charlie's mind, too.

"Lizzie, you have to come back for the launch. I can't do this myself. I'm counting on you. These are your babies. This is your book. This was your idea."

"I refuse to feel guilty, Charlie. I don't think I can

be in the same room as Jack."

Jack, I'm going to kill you. As soon as I figure out what the hell you did to her.

Beads of perspiration dotted his hairline. "You won't have to see Jack at the launch. He left a message this morning that he won't be available for it. I don't care if he makes it or not. Your photos make stars of his buildings. The book is about your artistry; his is secondary. Please Liz. Come home. I don't know what happened between you and Jack, but I promise you, we will work it all out."

****

Lizzie straightened her back. Reasonable enough to separate her devotion to Charlie from her growing fury with his blood relative, Lizzie couldn't believe Jack would blow off his brother. She couldn't fathom Jack's behavior at all. Charlie was counting on them both. How could he desert his brother when he needed him?

She was done playing the injured virgin. What was she thinking? How could she let Jack or any man make her feel insignificant? She would be there for Charlie.

"Okay, Charlie. I'll make arrangements and let you know when I'll be back."

"Thank you, Lizzie. Thank you. You won't regret this. The book is beautiful. I'm very proud of it. I think you will be, too."

Lizzie wouldn't let Jack taint her feelings for Charlie. She stuffed the few things she'd bought to wear since the day after Christmas into a shopping bag, checked out via the television and left the hotel to visit Kay in the hospital.

****

Amazed with Kay's transformation in three days,

Lizzie smiled at her beloved friend. "You look so much better."

"I wish I could say the same for you. The dark circles under your eyes have dark circles. Have you been sleeping at all? Look at those pants. They're falling off you. Have you eaten?"

"I'm OK, mom." Lizzie dropped her shopping bag on the floor and sat in the yellowish green, vinyl bedside armchair.

"I just came to say goodbye for now. I have to get back for the book launch. Then I might put in for an assignment to Africa again. But I promise I'll call. Please promise me you'll send pictures of the babies at least once a week wherever I am."

I need to go, to put my mind on something other than him.

"Don't leave. I don't have a good feeling about this. Stay here with us."

"I can't. Charlie called. He needs me."

"Is everything all right now? Have you talked to Jack?"

"No, it's over with Jack," she replied, her voice dull. Her eyes stung from crying. She was all cried out. "He never called me back."

Standing, she bent over the bed and wrapped her arms around Kay. "Don't worry about me. I'll be all right. I have to run and catch a flight. I'll call."

Releasing the hug after a good squeeze, Lizzie left the room. She was not going to fall apart, preferring cold, hard facts. If all Jack wanted was sex, fine. She had enjoyed the sex, too.

****

Jack was tired of sitting on the wood deck, staring

at the lake. His muscles ached from chopping the year's supply of logs stacked on the back porch. His grandfather's cabin offered him all the solitude he thought he needed. But after three days of mind-numbing brooding, he was no closer to solving his problems and was more depressed now than when he first arrived. No matter how he tried to free his mind of Beth, she had burrowed in and refused to release her hold on him.

Noting the caller ID on his cell phone when it rang, he picked up.

"Yes, Eileen. What is it?"

"I'm sorry to bother you, sir, but I have two urgent messages. The first is from Charlie, again. The second is from a Ms. Kay Lynch."

"What was the message from Kay?" He listened as Eileen read the message word for word. "Did she leave a number?" Jack scribbled down the number Eileen recited. "Okay, thanks. Did Ms. Moran call again?"

He was disappointed when his secretary told him, no. Damn it. It was like the day his mother left. Checking the mail every day, staring out the window.

"I'm not sure when I'll be heading back. I'll get in there and sign the papers you need soon. Thanks for everything, Eileen."

Grabbing a cold beer from the fridge, he dialed Kay's number suspecting he'd need alcoholic courage to deal with her. He was right.

"What the hell are you doing to Lizzie?" Kay lashed out at him. "What is wrong with you? How could you break her heart like that? I thought we understood each other. I told you about Lizzie's past because I thought you cared about her. I would never

232

have betrayed her confidence if I knew you only planned to hurt her with the information."

"Maybe she should have kept her past in the past." Jack wouldn't let an angry female intimidate him. He was angrier.

"Excuse me. You have a minute to explain yourself and the clock starts now."

"I don't know why you're so mad at me. I'm the one who got kicked in the gut."

"The clock's ticking, and I haven't heard an explanation."

He ran out of patience. "Why don't you ask Beth? She can tell you how she was in Wally's arms. She didn't know I saw them, but I did. Wally looked me right in the eye before he dove in for a long, juicy kiss."

Talking about it opened up the wound again. He hated the nagging pain from losing her, the conclusion that he was a jerk because she was never his to lose.

"I was going to give Beth the benefit of the doubt after she left me a message about the babies. By the way, congratulations." No reason to forget that Kay'd had a hard, dangerous time bringing her babies into the world.

"I called her back at the same number and got Wally's voice mail. Cozy, huh? I'm not stupid, Kay. If Beth wants Wally, although I think she's an idiot, it's a free country. I love her, Kay. I want her to be happy. There, are you happy now? Can you leave me alone?"

"No, I'm not going to leave you alone. *You're* the idiot, Jack. Wallace looked you right in the eye? Could it be that Wally was playing you and Lizzie? She told me he made a move on her again in front of the nursery. It made her mad as hell. Is that where you saw them?"

She didn't wait for him to tell her yes. He had the distinct impression she already knew she was right.

"Maybe you should have stuck around long enough to see Lizzie slap him away. God, you *are* an idiot, Jack. There is nothing between them. She's in love with you, and if I'm not mistaken she even told you so. She thinks there's something wrong with her because of the way you treated her. You abandoned her just like Wallace did. You don't deserve her any more than he does. He's a pompous ass. And you're a jackass, Jack."

It all rang true, and he had let that asshole best him. Who was the asshole, now?

"You may be right, Kay. But I thought she wanted Wally, not me. It drove me crazy to see her in his arms. That bastard. He did this to her, not me."

"You'll get no sympathy from me. You don't deserve her. I just kissed her goodbye. You have no idea how much you've made her suffer. What are you going to do about it?"

"Where is she? I need to make this right. I love her, Kay."

"She's traveling back to Chicago today. After Charlie assured her that you wouldn't be there, she agreed to go to the book launch on New Year's Eve. She plans to leave the next day for an open visit to Africa. I think she's running like she did when Wallace broke her heart, and I don't like it one damn bit."

"I can run fast Kay. I'll catch her. Thank you for setting me straight."

"You hurt her again, Jack, and I'll be your worst nightmare."

"I promise you. I will make this up to her. You have my word."

Chapter Twenty-One

Charlie had considered every detail to make the launch party a success; the setting in the penthouse floor of the JPH Building was perfect for a New Year's Eve bash. The three glass walls of the main conference room on the eastern façade of the building would give his guests an enviable view when the fireworks over the lake started at midnight.

Jack's assistant, Eileen, was a formidable organizer accepting each suggestion or requirement Charlie expressed with willing grace. She whipped every resource into shape, directed the men who moved office furniture off the floor and supervised the placement of abundant food and drink stations. She helped him with menu selections and selected the caterer who was semi-running between stations, overseeing set-up.

Yes, he had considered every detail of the event from every angle. Except, apparently, for one.

The launch of a coffee table book of the works of a single photographer required the photographer to be present. And she wasn't. Charlie was afraid to look at his watch again. It would only countdown to miserable failure if she didn't show up soon. Overheated, he pulled at his collar. Lizzie was giving him high blood pressure. He prayed to God that she'd arrive soon.

Despite the busywork from numerous distractions, he focused on the elevator door. He noticed the car moving upward as the floor numbers lit in sequence. Access to this floor for JP Hamilton Associates was via private elevator. Whoever was on that elevator was definitely coming here.

Charlie mumbled pleas to Mari and all the saints that Lizzie was a passenger on that car. When the doors opened with an airy swish, he was saved, redeemed.

Lizzie looked lovely in a short, unadorned long-sleeved dress of rose silk. Her sun-streaked hair was twisted up, the ends sprayed loose, shiny dark brown, streaked with copper and gold. She wore simple diamond studs as her only jewelry.

Charlie marveled at how gracefully she walked toward him in skyscraper high heels. He embraced her in a rush of euphoric relief. Tiny and fragile in his arms, he feared a healthy hug would crush her. He reared back to take a good look at her, and his stomach fell at the look in her eyes.

He had seen that look in the mirror every day until recently. She was grieving for Jack. Charlie was guilty as hell knowing he had exposed her to Jack.

"You had me so worried, Lizzie." Wanting to comfort her, Charlie put his arm around her shoulders. "I'm so glad to see you." He looked around the room. "What do you think of all this?"

****

Lizzie linked one arm around Charlie's waist and leaned toward him for support as she looked around. This was Jack's place. After being in his home, she'd know this was his even if the building didn't bear the firm's name. He'd left his mark here just like he'd left it on her. Her first time in his office would also be the last.

The thought broke her heart. She managed a weak smile, "I think all of this is fabulous, Charlie. You really are brilliant." She hugged him.

Charlie led her to an inner office to show her the finished book. When she realized where she was, she couldn't focus on the pages that Charlie was turning in front of her. No mistaking Jack's office. It had to be. There was a picture of Jack and Charlie together.

And diplomas.

She didn't know he went to Harvard grad school.

Another thing she didn't know about him that he had kept hidden from her.

A framed, autographed, Walter Payton jersey hung on the wall, too.

Love ya, Sweetness, but go Pack.

Charlie still talked and turned pages happily while her agitation mounted. Being here, where Jack seemed near, made his absence at this event a glaring insult to her. And to Charlie.

Her anger with Jack affirmed her decision to be there for Charlie even if his cold, selfish brother wouldn't.

"I'm so proud of you, Charlie. Let's go party."

Feeling self-satisfied, she mingled with the guests who unpacked in bunches from the elevator car. She talked up the book and praised the architectural genius of the man behind the buildings, without a hint of rancor. For Charlie's book, Jack was no more than window dressing.

Stronger by the minute, she went through the formalities of the evening, capable and happy that she could forget about Jack in personal terms even while extolling his professional virtues. He wasn't here and he didn't matter.

A voice that made her heart shake came from behind her. Jack.

Her internal pep talk tapered off as she faced him and knew in her heart that he did matter. She stared at him and forced her face to remain impassive, while heat and longing, hurt and unmitigated fury raged inside her. Her hand shook as she put her full champagne glass on a passing waiter's tray. Without a word, she pivoted and walked away from him.

He caught up with her easily and blocked her path. "We need to talk."

"I have nothing to say to you. Just leave me alone." Cornered, she scanned the crowded room for an escape route.

Jack moved closer, his large body hulking inches away and barred her from slipping past him.

"We need to talk." He grasped her arm.

"I don't want to hear what you have to say. Let me go," she hissed.

"Never."

Lizzie needed to get as far away from him as possible. Being in such close proximity to him played havoc with every one of her senses. "I *don't* want to talk to you." She jerked her arm free of his hold with little resistance.

Jack lowered his head and whispered, "We're making a bit of a scene, Beth."

Looking at the floor Lizzie whispered, "I am not making a scene. Just leave me alone."

She raised her head and met his eyes. "Don't ruin this night for Charlie. He worked so hard. Even if you seem to have forgotten how difficult it is for him, I haven't. He needs support, and that's the only reason I'm here. Still, if I had known that you were going to be here, I wouldn't have come."

His jaw clenched, his blue eyes darkened. "Just hear me out. Give me a few minutes. After I have my say, if you still want to go, I won't stop you."

Oh get it over with. A few more minutes in his company and it would all be over. She nodded, yes.

Gesturing for him to follow her, she stalked out of the reception area and led him to his office. He walked in behind her. She closed the door to end the questioning stares their earlier exchange had attracted.

Facing him, she folded her arms across her chest, and stared, unblinking. "What do you want from me? A repeat performance so you can leave me again? I don't think so. What is the old saying? Hurt me once, shame on you?"

"Beth, I'm sorry. I didn't mean to hurt you."

"Really? You weren't really trying? Just imagine what you could have done if you had given it your all."

Her heart pounding, she continued, "Just tell me one thing, Jack. Was it worth it? Was beating Wallace on a personal level as satisfying as on a professional one? Was stooping to his level worth it to you?"

Tears threatened to fall but she willed them away. She refused to cry in front of him. "I can't do this anymore. I'm leaving."

Lizzie tried to bull her way past him, but he grabbed her arm again and pulled her stiffening body against his.

"How could you ever think that I would stoop to Wally's level?"

She stopped struggling and gazed at the floor.

His lips moved against the top of her head. "I was a fool."

"I hope you're not waiting for me to disagree with you."

Releasing her, his fingers under her chin tipped her head up. "I was at least hoping you'd change that expression on your face."

Staring at him straight-faced, she drummed her fingers on her arm, and didn't change a thing.

"I saw red when I saw you in Wally's arms…" His voice wavered.

"Wally's arms? What the hell are you talking about?" She paced a few steps away, reversed and faced him. "Do you really think I could have given myself to you so willingly with Wallace still in my heart? What a low opinion you have of me. When did you see me in his arms?"

"Sit?" Jack gestured to a chair tucked under the front of his desk and she nodded.

Dragging two chairs over to the center of the room, Lizzie sat on one; Jack took a seat in front of her. "I missed you after you left my place Christmas Eve, and I came by yours to surprise you with coffee. I saw Marty with the little girl next door. She told me where you had gone. I decided to be with you and Kay for the big event."

He missed me? "Did you ever make it there? Why didn't I see you?"

Elbows on his thighs he leaned toward her. "Yes, I made it there. The first thing I saw when I got to the maternity floor at the hospital was you and Wally in a passionate embrace. Ring a bell?"

Lizzie resisted refuting the phrase "passionate

embrace," curious. "Did Wally know you were there?"

"He sure did," he replied wryly.

Clear now. *That worm can't be trusted.*

But Jack should know that he can trust me. "If you had stayed long enough, you would have seen my reaction to that one-sided *passionate embrace*," she related sarcastically. "Or if you had trusted me you wouldn't have needed to see me slap him away to know that I wouldn't cheat on you. But you didn't trust me enough."

"I'm sorry." His expression was humble with no trace of his usual over-confidence.

"Why didn't you trust me?"

"I don't know. Something snapped. I've never let any woman…get to me. I've seen what loving someone can do. Look at Charlie, Dad. None of that mattered when it comes to you."

He wet his lips. "You have to believe me. Beth, I love you."

Sitting erect, he held his hands toward her palms up, and she placed her hands in his, thrilling at the encompassing warmth of his touch. The passion in his blue eyes made her heart race. "It's that complicated and that simple. I'm a fool for you. I've never loved like this before, never told a woman I loved her. Only you, Beth. Only you."

Her heart leaped, elated, as tears welled. "I love you, too."

He drew her arms forward, kissed each hand and linked them behind his neck. With his hands around her waist, he pulled her off the seat to stand before him. As he buried his head against her abdomen, her every nerve ending tingled. He stood and Lizzie looked up into his navy blue eyes tenderly.

"I don't want you to run away to Africa. Stay with me," he implored.

"What?" Twisting away, she strode toward the window and stared at the city lights, his footsteps behind her.

Is that what I planned to do? Run away? No. Not this time.

She spun around and confronted him. "It's my job and I love it. Where did you get the impression that I was *running away?"*

"I talked to Kay."

Lizzie glared at him. "Look, Jack—"

A powerful sweep of his arms crushed her against his chest. His mouth covered hers, delicious, teasing the fight out of her. For seconds she luxuriated in the kiss, floating dreamlike on this potent current of attraction.

The kiss ended, and she opened her eyes, studying his face.

"You go wherever, whenever you like. Just always come back to me," he pleaded. "Do you forgive me, Beth?"

Lizzie could only nod and let the tears fall.

Heaving a sigh, he dug in his pocket. "One other thing. I never got the chance to give you your Christmas present."

He handed her a wrapped box. She tore the wrapping paper off, opened the velvet jeweler's box and laughed when she saw her gift: two tickets to a Green Bay Packer playoff game at Lambeau Field.

Lizzie chuckled. "A man who admits he's a fool and gives Packer tickets as a gift? I just might have to marry the boy."

"You just might." Jack took something out of his pocket and cupped it in his hand. Her gaze riveted on his midnight blue eyes, then down on his hand. Slowly he uncurled his fingers revealing an heirloom ring in his palm.

Love shining in his eyes, Jack beamed her a smile and slipped it on her trembling finger.

A word about the author...

K.M. Daughters is the pen name for team writers and sisters Pat Casiello and Kathie Clare. The pen name is dedicated to the memory of their parents, "K"ay and "M"ickey Lynch. K.M. Daughters is the author of twelve award-winning romance genre novels. The "Daughters" are wives, mothers, and grandmothers residing in the Chicago suburbs and on the Outer Banks, North Carolina. Visitors are most welcome at http://www.kmdaughters.com

Thank you for purchasing
this publication of The Wild Rose Press, Inc.

If you enjoyed the story, we would appreciate your
letting others know by leaving a review.

For other wonderful stories,
please visit our on-line bookstore at
www.thewildrosepress.com.

For questions or more information
contact us at
info@thewildrosepress.com.

The Wild Rose Press, Inc.
www.thewildrosepress.com

Stay current with The Wild Rose Press, Inc.

Like us on Facebook

https://www.facebook.com/TheWildRosePress

And Follow us on Twitter
https://twitter.com/WildRosePress